## "She's having the baby! I need help. *Fast.*"

Cecily felt like moaning. Eros had shot an arrow straight to her crotch. One look at Will and her heart had dropped to the tips of her unpedicured toenails. God help her, had he ever aged well.

Memories flooded back. That hair, short and tousled now. His shoulders had broadened and they held up a loose-fitting, short-sleeved white polo shirt that showed off muscled arms and a spectacular tan. Stone-colored pants hung casually off tight buns.

A shiver ran down her thighs. She felt hot and wet, and couldn't stem the sudden attack of heavy, dreamy lethargy. One look at him and she'd fallen for him again—drippily, stickily in lust with a married man.

Dear Reader,

Speaking as one who has an out-the-car-window relationship with cows, I can easily see how life as a big-animal veterinarian in rural Vermont could have its limitations, even if you had eleven cats to keep you company. So I understood why Cecily Connaught would view an obligatory wedding weekend in Dallas as her time to break out, have a fling with a stranger. Nor was it difficult to imagine that Will Murchison, no matter how much he wants to be Cecily's weekend fling, could get a little distracted by the missing groom, his client, whom he suspects of tax evasion.

But how can these two encounter a host of problems, conflicting life goals and continual interruption and still manage to fall in love, all in twenty-four hours? Read on....

Cheers!

*Barbara Daly*

P.S. Share your twenty-four-hour romance story with me at bdalybooks@aol.com.

## Books by Barbara Daly

# BARBARA DALY

## KISS & RUN

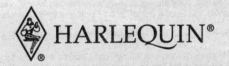

HARLEQUIN®

TORONTO • NEW YORK • LONDON
AMSTERDAM • PARIS • SYDNEY • HAMBURG
STOCKHOLM • ATHENS • TOKYO • MILAN • MADRID
PRAGUE • WARSAW • BUDAPEST • AUCKLAND

In loving memory of my own Cecily, who gave her family sixteen years of pure pleasure and unconditional love.

ISBN 0-373-69218-8

KISS & RUN

www.eHarlequin.com

Printed in U.S.A.

# 1

"KEEP THE CHANGE."

"But lady, it's a—"

"Smallest the ATM had." Cecily Connaught got a grip on her luggage, leaped out of the taxi and ran hell-for-leather into the church foyer, narrowly avoiding collision with a person hauling a chicken-wire structure out of a florist's van. Once inside, she halted for a moment, dizzied by the whirlwind of activity that surrounded her.

"Cecily, is that you?" Elaine Shipley's eyes were wide as she darted toward Cecily.

"Now is not the time for chit-chat," said a woman wearing peach who followed closely behind Elaine. "You're late," she told Cecily.

"At least she's here," said Elaine, "which is more than I can say for—"

"Now is not the time for gossip," said the woman in peach. "Get out of those shoes and put these on."

"But—" Apparently now was also not the time for protests. Someone took the bags out of her hands, sat her down, stripped off her comfortable, clunky sandals and slid her feet into a pair of mother-of-pearl satin stilettos—instant Misery by Manolo.

"You must rehearse in the shoes," Miss Peach said firmly, hauling Cecily to her feet. "We don't want any klutziness going down the aisle tomorrow. Now that you're here we have to get started," she muttered. "I don't give a damn who else is missing."

She got a tourniquet-strength hold on Cecily's arm and rushed her over to a group of women. Cecily took one look at them and segued from dazed to fashion-panicked. They were perfectly made up and coiffed and were wearing cute little skirts, short but not too short, that showed off endless, thin, tanned legs and were topped with belly shirts that revealed flat, tanned tummies. In the long, droopy bachelor's-button-printed sundress she'd bought at the Blue Hill Thrift Shop when Vermont had an unprecedented heat wave and it got too hot for jeans, she was hands down the worst dressed among them. Her careless appearance explained Elaine Shipley's wide eyes. If Cecily's mother had been there, she would have died of shame.

But then, her mother had vegetated into a person who was incapable of understanding any choice Cecily made, especially her choice to be a veterinarian instead of a—fashion designer, maybe?

"The maid of honor," Miss Peach said with a note of triumph in her voice, "is present and accounted for."

A dark-haired beauty at the center of the group, whirled, and her eyes widened just as her mother's had. "Cecily? Cecily!" she said and pulled Cecily into a bear hug.

The bride, Sally Shipley, daughter of Elaine, was dressed even more sedately than her entourage and even more perfectly pulled together. Cecily got as far as saying, "Sally, it's been a long—" before Miss Peach, who had to be the wedding planner, interrupted.

"No time for reminiscence." Much like a gravel truck, she scooped up all of them and hustled them down the aisle, shoving them into place. "Leave a space," she said to Cecily. "The matron of honor hasn't shown up yet. Reverend Justice," she commanded the cleric who already stood facing an imaginary crowd, "go for it. I'll bring in the others when they choose to grace us with their presence." Her voice dripped annoyance.

The bride grabbed her groom by the elbow. "This is Gus," she whispered to Cecily.

Cecily held out a hand. "Nice to meet—"

"No introductions *now.*" Miss Peach practically yelled the words, then sprinted up the aisle.

Sally meekly turned toward the minister, who intoned, "Dearly beloved..."

Feeling dizzy and disoriented, Cecily shifted her weight from one aching foot to the other. The rest of the wedding party might be dearly beloved by each other, but she wasn't even dearly beloved by the bride, whose maid of honor she'd foolishly agreed to be. *Barely remembered* was more like it.

But however reluctant to be in the wedding of a woman she hadn't been friends with since they were five years old, she now had a mission, one she could start on while the wedding party was...

"...gathered here today to share with Sally and Gus that most sacred moment when they join their lives in holy—"

*Hell.* Marriage was such a crock. It was a mistake Cecily didn't intend to make. She'd never do what her mother had done—give up a career to marry a man who largely ignored her.

Her father. He didn't understand Cecily's choices, either, the only difference being that he didn't particularly care. He loved only one thing, making...

"…that most honored of all commitments, most binding of all vows, to love, honor and cherish…"

…news in the academic world by writing brilliant papers in his field, finance. Her mother had wanted her to be a socialite. Her father had wanted her to go into marketing. No wonder she'd chosen to hang with cows.

Cecily took a deep, calming breath. She was in a bad mood because her mother had conned her into accepting Sally's maid-of-honor position. Because she'd had to get up at four this morning in the frosty cold of May in Vermont to make it to the searing heat of May in Dallas for the rehearsal. But most of all because the four-inch heels with long, witchy toes were killing her feet. Not even a mature, professional woman, a large-animal vet, for heaven's sake, could go from thirty degrees to ninety-plus, from Teva sandals to torture devices, and still stay grounded.

But as Sally's maid of honor, she had to act nice. She'd always acted nice, and this was no time for a personality change. Besides, this was merely the rehearsal. Sally, who was doing the wedding two-step for the second time around—as if the disastrous first time hadn't taught her a lesson—still had twenty-four hours to come to her senses. With any luck, Cecily might be able to kiss these shoes goodbye after one wearing.

And she had her mission to accomplish. There'd once been a boy who might have changed her mind about love and marriage, and with any luck at all, he was here right now, standing in the line of groomsmen winging out behind Gus. Through pure serendipity, this weekend might be her second chance with him. She zeroed in on the last groomsman in the line.

He had bleached light blond hair cut short and charmingly disheveled. Blue eyes. Stone-colored chinos—Hugo Boss. White polo shirt—Calvin Klein. Burgundy loafers—Gucci—no socks. She knew the designers because the logo was visible on each piece of clothing. He was cute but definitely not Will Murchison. Too bad.

It wasn't that she was hoping she and Will would fall in love and start planning their own wedding. Now that she was a sensible, career-oriented adult, she was determined never to marry, never to make the mistake her mother had made, giving up her own career in business to follow her father from one university position to a better one. All Cecily wanted was a weekend fling with a boy—a man by now— she had, for some odd reason, never quite forgotten.

The memory had come back like the crash of waves on the shore when she had finally, on the plane this morning, looked at the wedding itinerary and seen Will's name on the list of groomsmen. That boy's name was Will Murchison. She'd heard him say he was from Dallas, and until the afternoon in the groundskeeper's cottage, the most exciting thing he'd ever said to her was, "I rode her pretty hard. Give her a good rubdown, okay?"

He'd been talking about a horse. He was a senior at Exeter, the prestigious boys' school, while she was a senior at a day school in Boston and, because she was already intrigued by the idea of being a veterinarian, worked weekends at the stables where he rode.

She hadn't said more than two words to him. She might have opened a conversation by telling him she'd been born in Dallas, for heaven's sake. She might have mentioned that her parents still had friends there. She might have dropped the names of those friends, looking for a connection, and they would probably have found one. But no. She was too shy, too awed by him, to do anything but goggle and occasionally stammer, "You're welcome," because he always said, "Thanks," with a smile that shot heat through her from head to toe.

She eyed Groomsman Number Three, looking for that sexy smile. Blue eyes. Khaki chinos—Calvin Klein. Yellow polo shirt—Lacoste. Sandals—more Gucci. No socks, naturally. Was it possible his hair had blond highlights? But no sexy smile. He wasn't Will, either. The odds were diminishing.

Will had usually been surrounded by a gaggle of horse-crazy, man-crazy girls, but that stormy afternoon when she'd been sent out to find him on the trail and lead him to shelter, they'd been alone, and he'd tried to kiss her. Instead of accepting a dream come true and kissing him back, whatever the cost, she'd fled out into the storm. The school year had ended and she'd never seen him again. And nobody like him—oozing with an overabundance of adolescent testosterone and still kind and mature for his age—had come along to take his place.

She looked over the second groomsman. Dirty-blond hair and *green* eyes. The sunglasses perched on top of his head had the Gucci logo on the earpiece. He wore running gear that was covered in logos and sweat and, like her, he wasn't paying attention to the minister. He was too absorbed in his cool-down stretches.

All the groomsmen had fashion-victim facial hair, Numbers Three and Four with cheeks unshaven and Number Two with a manicured goatee.

They all looked alike, but none of them looked in the least like the Will she remembered. Murchison was an important Texas name. There might be dozens of Will Murchisons. Now disappointment washed through her. But in front of Groomsman Number Two was a wide, empty space. The wedding planner had said something about people missing. There was still hope.

Faint hope. Will had come into her life a gazillion years ago, but she hadn't been able to stop herself from thinking *what if.* What if she'd let him kiss her? The psychiatrist her mother had forced her to see had said she was using the memory of him as an excuse not to get involved with anyone else and had suggested in a most un-Freudian way that Cecily should *get over it.*

Obedient as always, she had. She was happy with her life's plan—a successful career and a succession of lovers. The career part was going fine. As for the succession of lovers, she was tanking. And that, of course, was why she'd been so excited to see Will's name on the roster of wedding attendants.

If they connected this weekend, there was always the possibility she might be able to use the opportunity to catch up on her sex life. It wasn't shoes, sleepiness or submission to her mother's will after all, she decided. It was her deprived and complaining libido that had put her in a bad mood.

But what if Will did show up among the missing? Why hadn't she spent a little time in New York checking out current fashion and then bought some of it? And some decent underwear! She shuddered just thinking about the white cotton bras and panties she bought three to a pack at the Ben Franklin store in Blue Hill, Vermont. This might be her chance to…

"…embark on that ship of love that will sail them to the shores of supreme happiness…"

…and she wasn't prepared! She cast another glance at the beautiful bridesmaids, the gorgeous groomsmen. These were Will's type of people. She sighed. She didn't have a chance.

At least the church was pretty—St. Andrews, favored for weddings by Dallas brides, Cecily's mother had told her. The early afternoon Texas sun shone through the stained-glass windows, tinting the bridesmaids' pale shoes petal pink and bathing their sharp-featured faces with a rosy glow. The scent of vetiver-scented soaps and aftershave drifted in Cecily's direction from the collection of groomsmen, while light, summery perfumes emanated from the bridesmaids, as though to compete with the flowers that would soon fill the church.

It was an exquisite scene, but not a serene one. The chaos continued, even increased in motion and volume. Miss Peach dispatched her army of minions hither and yon. A photographer fiddled with lights and tripods in the balcony overlooking the sanctuary. The good-looking man scribbling on a pad must be a reporter. Sally's mother stood at the back of the church, wringing her hands. Of course, three members of the wedding party were missing the rehearsal, and Gus— tall, broad-shouldered, as heavily muscled as an ox and at the moment, looking tense—appeared capable of murdering all of them. She hoped Sally hadn't married the Mob. Cecily supposed that was enough to make a mother of the bride wring her hands.

Listening to the minister drone on, sounding as if even he didn't believe a word he was saying, she swallowed a yawn of the most graceless magnitude.

It was too bad she'd known Sally since they were tiny, adorable babies in breathtakingly expensive dresses, Sally looking like a dark-haired devil, Cecily a blond angel—not that Cecily remembered, but her mother had sent a packet of pictures to jog her memory. It was also too bad that Sally, known to be the wild child in her group of friends—a fact sorrowfully confided by her mother to Cecily's mother— would suddenly reveal her sentimental streak and invite her *first* friend rather than her *best* friend to be her maid of honor.

Even in an unaccustomed fit of sentimentality, how could inviting Cecily to be in the wedding have crossed Sally's mind? By the time they were five their interests had taken them in different directions— Sally to ballet, Cecily to horseback riding. That, plus the fact that Cecily's father had moved from Southern Methodist University to Purdue, the first of a string of moves, meant she and Sally hadn't been close friends since they were five and hadn't seen each other since they were sixteen.

But through all those moves, Cecily's mother had never lost a friend. Thus it was embarrassingly possible she had suggested to Sally's mother that since Sally was dead set on leaving her wild reputation behind when she married Gus, inviting her first friend to be her maid of honor would convey that impression— something the wedding reporter might pick up on.

Cecily had tried saying no, that she couldn't leave Vermont during calving season. Her mother, who'd joined the Mothers in Support of Offspring Guilt Club upon moving to New York, had called to say weepily, "Don't you care about anything but cows? Can't you give a passing thought to your family and—"

"...friends are here to witness their vows and share their happiness as they embark upon..."

*A dangerous sea in a rickety boat.* That's what marriage was. But Cecily had capitulated, although she hadn't been happy about it.

"Do you, Gus Hargrove, take Sally Shipley to be..."

If Will appeared, if he showed even the slightest flicker of interest, she'd take him in a New York minute! As far as she could tell, an available, compatible man didn't exist in Blue Hill or points nearby. To require the services of a large-animal vet, a man apparently had to be married, preferably a long time, therefore both married and old. She worked so hard that these were the only men she came in contact with—plus Dr. Vaughn, of course, but not only was he older and more married than any of his clients, Maddie Vaughn had become Cecily's surrogate mother. So the part of the plan that involved having a string of casual lovers had reached desperation point. She hadn't had a date, much less sex, for three years.

A long, steamy twenty-four hours in Dallas stretched in front of her like an invitation to wild and uninhibited behavior. No one in Blue Hill would ever know that their own Dr. Connaught, respected veterinarian, was a tightly leashed tigress inside.

"I do," Gus said.

"Instead of the traditional vows, Sally will read a poem she wrote in honor of this, the most important event in her life."

"Your eyes delight me," Sally began in a Miss America voice, gazing passionately into Gus's eyes, which shifted away uneasily. "Your lips excite me," she continued, and Gus's mouth tightened. "Your love ignites me..."

*Oh, for chrissakes.* Sally's father should have hired somebody to write that poem. Maybe he had. A very bad poet. Mr. Shipley should ask for his money back, because—

"Sorry, sorry, sorry." The voice came like thunder from the back of the church, and Cecily whirled against an imminent lightning bolt.

"Will!" Sally shrieked. "You're late, you turkey. Where's Muffy?"

"She didn't make it. She's having the baby. I need help. *Fast.*"

Mrs. Shipley's moan was audible from the back of the church.

Cecily felt as if she might moan, too. Eros had shot an arrow straight to her crotch. One look at Will and her heart had dropped to the tips of her unpedicured, possibly not even clean, toenails. God help her, had he ever aged well.

Memories flooded back as he gave Sally a warm hug and Gus a manly slap on the shoulder. That hair, short and tousled now, the silky red-brown of a fine Santa Gertrudis bull. His shoulders had actually broadened and they held up a loose-fitting, short-sleeved white polo shirt that showed off muscled arms and a spectacular tan. Stone-colored pants hung casually off tight buns. The pants had a logo across one pocket. It said Ralph Lauren.

As he talked to Sally, Cecily got a profile view of his eyelashes, as long as the bridesmaids' skirts. Unlike the groomsmen, his only facial hair was his thick, glossy chestnut eyebrows. Not a fashion victim, even if he was wearing pants with a logo, which she'd forgive.

A shiver ran down her thighs. She felt hot and wet, and swayed rhythmically from a sudden attack of heavy, dreamy lethargy. Here he was, the prize bull of her dreams, and she'd lassoed him too late. He wasn't merely married, he was about to be a daddy.

She wanted to burst into loud sobs.

"Call the po-po," chirped the bridesmaid with the perfect navel. Cecily swiveled to stare at her. She'd meant 911, surely.

Will swiveled, too. "I did that already. I'm telling you the baby's coming *right now,* in my car, in the church parking lot!" He raised his voice to include everybody in the church. "Is there a doctor in the house? Anybody with medical experience or first aid—"

"Cecily," Sally said, grabbing her arm and pushing her toward this frantic Will person. "Cecily can deliver the baby."

"Cecily?" Will said in a suddenly hushed voice, and his gaze locked directly on her. "From the Green Trails Stable?" His hazel eyes glinted with gold and they were filled with some emotion Cecily didn't care to explore. She hated to think what her eyes were saying to him.

It was more than she could bear. Cecily spun away from those marvelous eyes to hiss at Sally. "No, I can't. I'm a vet, not a—"

"Don't tell Muffy," Sally snarled back.

"Cecily Connaught," Will went on in that distracted voice. "I can't believe it really is you. After all these—"

He'd remembered her name, her entire name. Cecily leaned toward Sally's ear, anything to keep from looking at Will. "It might even be illegal."

Sally practically spat into Cecily's opposite ear. "Muffy's a bitch. You're a vet. What's illegal?" Then she wheeled them both into positions flanking Will. "How nice you've already met. Get going."

Mrs. Shipley sped forward, wringing her hands even more violently. "But Sally—"

"Chill, Mama."

"So, you've become a doctor?" Will didn't seem inclined to move.

"Catch up on old times later! Have you forgotten the baby? This is an emergency!" Sally sounded a lot like Miss Peach.

"Right," Will said, taking his eyes off Cecily at last. "It *is* an emergency." Suddenly purposeful, he grabbed Cecily while Sally—the snake—slithered back up to the altar and Mrs. Shipley shrank into a pew and sank limply onto the cushion. "All of you stay here," Cecily said over her shoulder quite unnecessarily, since nobody seemed to be rushing forward to help, either from the wedding party or the mob in the foyer. "The fewer spectators, the better." Her words trailed away on the breeze she and Will made as he propelled her through the foyer crowd and out the doors of the chapel into the glaring sun. "Wait a minute, wait a minute—"

"We don't have a minute." He sounded grim.

"My bag's in the church foyer. I need it."

Cecily felt the jolt when he halted. "You brought your medical bag to the wedding rehearsal?"

"Had to come here straight from the airport. I never travel without it." She spared a second to wonder why. Had she thought a horse might turn up in first class needing a tracheotomy?

"Oh." They reversed direction and he whizzed her back into the church, where she swooped down and gripped the bag without losing speed, and then they were off again toward the parking lot, racing past limousines, the florist's van and enough BMWs to start up a dealership.

Her shoes weren't made for running. She was in agony. "Has it been a normal pregnancy?" she said, thinking ahead.

"Far as I know."

"Full term?"

"Apparently. The baby is coming."

It was clear he hadn't taken the proper interest in his wife's pregnancy. Maybe he'd grown up to be one of those men who only *looked* good. But oh, wow, did he ever look good.

"Here she is." He flung open the back door of a still-running luxurious gray sedan. A blast of icy air emerged along with a piercing scream.

*"Where have you been?* I'm about to drop a baby all by myself onto a church parking lot from the back seat of a freaking car!"

Together Cecily and Will leaned into the car. Cecily was shoulder to shoulder with the muscles, hip to hip with the tight buns, smelling the scent of a deliciously clean, very hot man. He turned to her with a desperate glance. They were nose to nose, eye to eye, and Eros was shooting arrows like a madman, zigzags that shot down through the center of her body. *Move over, Muffy, I'm the one who needs the back seat of this car.*

She felt the heat rise to her face. It had been an inappropriate thought, and fortunately no more than a thought. Will was looking at Muffy now, oblivious to anything other than the crisis at hand.

"Muffy." She could tell he was trying to be firm, but his voice wasn't totally steady. "I said let's go to the hospital, you said it was a false alarm, you said—"

Cecily whacked him on the elbow and, wonder of wonders, he got the message.

"Here's the doctor," he said, calm now and very gentle. "She'll take care of you."

Muffy raised herself up on one elbow and left off screaming long enough to puff a few times and then say, "You don't *look* like a doctor. Have you ever delivered a baby?"

"Many," Cecily said, taking a second out to put her hand on Muffy's flailing one, trying to make a connection with the woman before they got to the hard part. It worked with cows and horses in distress. Maybe it worked with bitches. "Keep up your breathing while I prep."

"Forget prep. Wash your hands and get on with it!" A long, pitiful wail emerged from a wide, carnivorous mouth as another contraction consumed her.

Cecily glanced at her big, chunky, utilitarian watch, starting to time the contractions. "Breathe, that's right, breathe. Puff, puff, puff…" She dived into her bag, wincing at the sight of the huge syringes, the Veterinary Purposes Only medications and the oversized forceps, got out the antibacterial wash, poured it over her hands and slid them into sterile gloves, then slid a sterile apron over her sundress. "I'm doing a quick exam. Don't push." In spite of herself, she'd said it pretty sharply, because Muffy was pushing like mad.

"Are…you…*insane*?" Muffy's words came out sporadically between puffs of breath. "If I don't push, how the hell am I going to get this thing out of me?"

Cecily reflected on the advantages of delivering calves. No cow had ever mooed at her in that tone of voice. Nor had she ever delivered a calf with the bull running around in tight little circles, clutching a cell phone to his ear. Nor had she ever lusted after the bull, but that was another story. Soothing, that was what she had to be. Calm and soothing. "If everything's fine, I'll tell you to push. Just hold back for a minute, okay? You," she said to the father-to-be, "hold her hand, help her with her breathing."

"Yeah, sure, that will do a lot of good, him holding my hand, helping me with my breathing. He tried to *smother* me once. Tell him to go away. He's making me dizzy."

"What do you mean *if* everything's fine?" That was Will, looking for something else to worry about.

"I want to be sure the head's coming this way, not the hooves."

"The *what?*" Muffy rose up on her elbows.

"A doctor joke," Cecily said, still struggling for calm and soothing. "I meant the feet, of course."

A loud shriek came from Muffy. A deep moan came from Will.

"The mother is often not herself during delivery," Cecily murmured to Will. "Don't take it personally."

"She *is* herself," Will said. "Muffy's a hater. Just deliver the baby, okay?"

"Righto," Cecily said, wondering if Will's marriage might be destined to end in divorce. Probably not. Men gravitated to bitches, confident in their ability to tame them. The worst of her lust attack was over, dimmed by the harrowing excitement of the impending birth as well as awareness of the futility of lusting after Will.

A sigh rose from deep inside her anyway. Oh, well, if she'd found Will too late to have his baby, she could sure as heck deliver it.

She didn't have time or the equipment to do an episiotomy. But Muffy was fully dilated and the baby was crowning, Cecily noted with great relief. "Now you can push," she told Muffy. "That's right, push, push, almost there. Come on, you're a trooper, you can do it—"

Simultaneously Muffy screamed at the top of her lungs and the baby came into the world with a healthy cry. "It's a girl!" Cecily said, swiftly clamping and cutting the umbilical cord, hoping the navel would equal the bridesmaid's in beauty and symmetry. And as the sound of sirens drowned out Muffy's shuddering sobs of relief, Cecily added, "A beautiful little girl and a fire truck, a police car…no, three police cars and—oh, wonderful—here at last are the EMTs, just when we need them least."

Cecily examined the baby while the paramedics gently lifted Muffy onto a stretcher and carried her toward the ambulance, ignoring the blistering she was giving them for taking so long to get there. Then Cecily handed over the child, explaining the conditions of the delivery as well as giving them a verbal checklist of what she had and hadn't done. At long last, the ambulance doors closed and blessed silence prevailed.

Alone in the parking lot, Cecily pulled off her gloves and apron, then wiped her forehead. She hadn't seen Will leave with Muffy, but he must have. A tear of regret dripped down her face and landed on the toe of one satin shoe, matching the splash of antiseptic on the other. Then she caught sight of another pair of shoes.

Loafers—Gucci. No socks. Her gaze traveled upward…on Will, who lay slumped against a tire.

She'd always heard this happened—new mother did fine and new father fainted—but she'd thought it was an amusing contemporary myth. Apparently not. She crouched down beside him. "Will. Will!" She grabbed his hands and began to massage his wrists with her thumbs, then took his pulse.

"What happened?" He sounded groggy, but he was apparently alive.

"The baby came."

"Oh. Good."

Cecily stifled an exasperated sound. "It's a girl."

"Mmm."

She raised her voice. "Mother and child are doing *fine*."

"I wish I were."

She'd had it. "Look," she said, thinking how wonderful it was not to need a verbal bedside manner in veterinary medicine, "your relationship with Muffy is none of my business, but this is one of those times you have to rise above your differences and support her. A woman who's just given birth feels very vulnerable. She needs you now." Cecily stood up. "So get your ass in gear. We're going to the hospital to see her, and I mean right this second."

She glared at him.

He stared at her.

"I'll drive," she said with a confidence she didn't feel. "Last thing in the world I would have expected you to be, but it seems you're a fainter."

He didn't look the least bit guilty about his disinterest, just puzzled. Still staring at her, he went around the car—Cecily noticed the distinctive Audi emblem—got in on the passenger side and maneuvered the seat so far back she couldn't see his face out of the corner of her eye.

But she could feel his eyes on her and allowed herself one sidelong glance at him as she adjusted the rearview mirror. God, he was sexy. Everything about him said male, male, *male*. His mouth was full and enticing. His eyes were hot. Suddenly feeling over-whelmed, she pushed the key into the ignition.

He settled his sunglasses into place, hiding what-ever message his eyes might have been sending, so she could let herself imagine that his gaze was an approv-ing one, could feel it wash over her like warm honey.

Honey, but no crumpet. One look at Will and she'd fallen for him again. This time she was drippily, stick-ily in lust with a married man.

# 2

WILL SETTLED INTO THE LEATHER upholstery of his new car, wondering what the hell was going on. Cecily had miraculously dropped into his life again after many, many years, and all she seemed able to think about was his and Muffy's relationship.

Maybe Sally had told her about Muffy. He'd never mentioned her at the stables, and for good reason. When they were growing up, he and Muffy had gotten along about as well as a Maine coon cat and a Yorkshire terrier, he being the terrier. It was one of the reasons their parents had sent him to Exeter. They'd thought it was time to get Will out from under her thumb.

It had worked, too. They were doing much better as adults. They hadn't sunk to physical violence since they were twenty-seven or so, although Muffy had been telling the truth when she'd said he'd tried to smother her once. When they were kindergarten age, he'd put a plastic bag over her head and attempted to tie it around her throat while she was sleeping. He'd done it because she'd sneered at him and said he'd never be popular in the neighborhood because he was about as exciting as phonics. He'd felt like killing her.

Not really. A thinking man, even at that early age,

he'd poked holes in the bag before he shoved it over her head. He'd just wanted to send the message, *Make fun of me again and you're toast.*

Muffy hadn't seen it that way.

When they were seven, their parents had taken them on a short car trip to the mountains of the Big Bend—a trial run, their mother had called it, to test whether or not the family could survive a major trip west the following year to see the Grand Canyon and Yosemite Park. Will still hadn't seen the Grand Canyon or Yosemite.

Years later, they'd made a pact to get through the holidays at their parents' house by not speaking to each other at all. Marrying Gator had softened Muffy some—at least toward Will, now that she had Gator to pick on—but they still didn't get together socially or as a family except under duress.

It was a miracle he didn't hate women.

He'd been a prince, a virtual *prince*, to pick her up in Waco and drive her to Dallas when Gator had to fly up to Fort Worth earlier in the week for a sports-equipment trade show. A less princely man would have chosen slow death by torture over being in a confined space with Muffy for a couple of hours.

He was doing it for Sally. Sally was their cousin and they'd lived through every second of her disastrous first marriage. Sure, she'd been a wild thing, a seriously dedicated playgirl, until she'd met Gus, fallen madly in love and sworn to change her ways. But she had a good heart. Which reminded Will that he had a family responsibility to make sure Gus was a man who would give Sally the happiness she deserved. And Will had reasons to feel concerned.

About the time Sally met Gus, he'd been looking

for a new tax man and Sally had recommended Will. As was customary at his accounting firm, Helpern and Ridley in Houston, since Will did the taxes for Gus's security business, he also filed Gus's personal returns. In March, looking at the numbers Gus had sent him, Will saw some discrepancies in Gus's reported income and his lifestyle. Will had put many hours of his own time into tracking down what Gus might have left out of his documentation and hadn't come up with a thing. Since Gus had done him the honor of asking him to be a groomsman, Will felt guilty as all hell accepting, knowing he'd be doing his best to pump Gus and his friends for information. But tax was his profession, damn it, and he had a professional obligation to make sure a tax return was honest and accurate before he signed his name to it.

He couldn't let Sally marry somebody engaged in something shady. He had twenty-four hours to satisfy himself about those discrepancies or he'd have to stop the wedding.

With no time to waste, Cecily was a distraction he didn't need. She was the girl from his past he'd never forgotten, the girl who wouldn't let him kiss her, a girl who *still*, after all these years had passed, didn't seem the slightest bit interested in him. Seeing her wouldn't have come as such a shock if he'd bothered to read the itinerary of events Sally and Gus had sent him. He might have prepared for it, thought up a few cool moves, a sophisticated line.

Sheltered behind his sunglasses, he gazed at her, at her straight little nose, her perfect skin, but pale now, no tan. No makeup, either. With the sun shining through her lashes, he could see they were long and light and slanted down instead of curling up. Her mouth was wide, a mouth made to smile, although she hadn't smiled much in the few minutes since she'd sprung so unexpectedly back into his life.

She still had the thick blond hair he remembered, a little darker now, more the color of honey. When she used to come down from Boston to work at the stables, it had been in a neat bob. Now it was long and sloppily tied at the nape of her neck, as if all she wanted was to get it out of the way. At the stables, her jodhpurs had been perfect, her shirts impeccable. She'd looked like the girls who attended the private schools near Exeter. But today she was wearing a shapeless flowered sundress. He liked the look. It was natural, unlike the look of most women who wandered in and out of his life these days. Cecily's dress left him wondering about the curves beneath it, let his imagination loose, and his imagination didn't fit the profile of an accountant's.

One thing hadn't changed. Her eyes were as wide and blue as they'd always been, that monitor-screen blue of a midday sky. From the first moment she'd handed him the reins of a horse, pinning him with those eyes, she'd appealed to him in some way he couldn't quite get a handle on. And she still did. So why the hell couldn't he get her to feel the same way about him?

Muffy, Muffy, Muffy. All she seemed to be able to think about. He had nothing to feel guilty about where Muffy was concerned. He'd been wallowing in his own self-righteousness until Cecily, who'd apparently become a doctor, had decided that delivering his niece, a simple act of professional mercy, gave her the right to tell him he *still hadn't done enough for Muffy.*

In fact, he hadn't. Not quite. "Which hospital are they taking her to?" he asked.

"Glen Oaks Care Center. Have you heard of it?"

"Sure," he said, already dialing Gator's cell, where he left a terse message, then dialed the number for Gator's plane. As he listened to the phone ring, he observed that while the doctor looked capable at the wheel—strong armed and steady—they still hadn't made it out of the church parking lot. "It's a small, private— Hey," he said when Gator answered, "she's at GOCC. Okay. Okay. O-kay, I'll do it. Yeah, see you."

"We need cigars," he told Cecily. "We'll stop on the way."

She did another one of those little whooshy sounds, like the one she'd done when he'd still been trying to get the blood running back to his head. "Do you happen to know where GOCC is?" she said, sounding like patience sitting on a pressure cooker.

"Yes."

"Would you consider sharing it with me?"

Uh-oh, a little steam was starting to show. She'd found the parking lot exit at last, and sat there poised, waiting for him to answer.

He saw a way to put off visiting Muffy indefinitely. "Left," he instructed her and punched the number two on his phone to direct his next call to his parents.

"Now what?" Cecily had reached an intersection.

"Take the LBJ."

"Okay." The car didn't move. "Where is it?"

"Take a right and follow the signs. I need to make these calls." When his mother answered, he said "Hi. You have a granddaughter." Interrupting the shrieks of excitement, the string of questions, he said, "Details later. She's at GOCC. Right. See you there."

Now he'd done everything anyone could have expected. Gator was about to take off from Meacham Field in Fort Worth. He'd be at Love Field in Dallas in the time it took a small plane to go straight up, then straight down. The proud Murchison grandparents, who lived in Highland Park, would beat Gator to the hospital. Muffy would soon be surrounded by people who actually liked her.

What he wanted to do now was renew his acquaintance with Cecily. What she wanted to do was take him straight to the hospital to see Muffy. Why was she so determined to make him visit the twin sister who, from the second he'd entered the world, had made his life a living hell?

CECILY HAD TO ADMIT THAT SHE was a little disappointed in the kind of man Will had apparently grown up to be. And she didn't mean a *married* man. If he had to be a married man, she wanted him to be a *good* married man. It was upsetting that he'd seemed so reluctant to follow his wife and baby to the hospital. Maybe he'd been in shock, because now, making his phone calls to family or friends, he sounded pleased and excited.

Driving Will's luxurious car made her intensely nervous. She was out of her element. Three years in the country and she'd already forgotten that in a city, even a parking lot could be hard to negotiate without a map. In Vermont, even the freeway was a gentle, comfortable, aesthetically pleasing experience. The LBJ, she feared, would be a jungle.

Seeing the first sign pointing toward it, she went

into panic mode. She'd never had a sense of direction, and she'd lost her freeway fighting skills. Those two things combined with the inappropriate feelings she had toward the man she was driving were a foolproof recipe for disaster. Still, getting Will to the hospital was a job she had to do, and she always did her job.

Uh-oh, she had to make a choice—head north and east or south and west. "Will," she said, "which direction do I go on the LBJ? Tell me quick, because northeast is the left lane and southwest is the right lane, and I don't know how the hell I'm going to change lanes."

Will sat back, folded his arms over his chest and said, "You're fine where you are."

What a relief. The traffic swarmed around her, cars cutting in front of her, sliding in behind her, but all she had to do was cling to her spot in this lane. It led her up the entrance ramp. She'd arrived. She was on the freeway. Standing still.

"Lots of traffic," she said.

"It's always like this," Will said.

"But we need to hurry!" She raised her hand to slam the heel onto the horn in the center of the steering wheel.

He grabbed her wrist. "Honking won't help."

The touch of his fingertips sent her into total meltdown. Will had turned her on to a degree she couldn't ignore. It was her own fault that she'd let it happen. If she'd only read on after she'd sighted Will's name, if she'd only noticed that a Muffy Murchison was also in the wedding party, she would have assumed the worst and accepted it with spartan stoicism. But she hadn't read on, and one look at him had her drooling on his shoes. Now she had to redirect her raging lust.

This frivolous trip to Dallas for Sally's wedding had become a landmark in her life. She'd buried herself so completely in her work that she'd forgotten the realities of life. She needed sex just as any normal woman did.

And she needed it now. She'd find somebody else to spend a hot, steamy twenty-four hours with, and Will could help her do it.

She'd delivered Will's baby. Now he, by golly, could deliver her into the arms of an *unmarried* man.


WILL WAS AFRAID HE'D MISSED his calling. He should have been a military strategist. While Cecily was hardly the enemy, his diversionary tactics had gotten her onto the LBJ going in the wrong direction, and the freeway was packed. Now that they were on it, they'd be here a while.

Which suited Will just fine because he'd be sitting beside Cecily, charming the pants off her, he hoped. It had been a long time since anybody had called him dull. In fact, from the time he'd left home for Exeter, he'd been amazed at the number of girls—now women—who wanted to go out with him. In those years away from Muffy he'd discovered he could be himself, not Muffy's stuffy twin brother, Will.

Cecily didn't know he'd *ever* been Muffy's stuffy brother. So why, when he'd tried to kiss her, had she run like a bunny out into a violent electrical storm?

It hadn't boosted his ego any. He'd eventually gotten over the ego part, so why hadn't he completely gotten over Cecily?

"We should be looking for the Glen Oaks exit." Which was actually where they'd gotten on the freeway. A full loop of Dallas in heavy traffic ought to give him time to have her eating out of his hand. Figuring it was time to set the scene for intimate conversation, he punched up a CD, turned the surround sound down low and searched for a conversation starter. "So, you came back for the wedding." *Brilliant, Will, just brilliant.*

"Under duress." The fine line of cheekbone and jaw tightened.

"You and Sally were friends somewhere along the way? I mean, obviously you were."

"When we were too young to know better."

"So, you lived in Dallas and then you moved away?" It was as if cracking a crab getting anything out of her. But that explained why he didn't know her. By junior high their group had been pretty tight, a clique that grew out of sharing a neighborhood, school and country club. Some of them didn't even like each other, but those things and family ties—their parents' friendships or business relationships—bound them together. Sally and Muffy, for example, were always at each other's throats, and yet Sally had asked Muffy to be her matron of honor.

To his surprise, Cecily suddenly got chatty. "My father's a professor of economics. I was born here while he was at SMU. We've moved numerous times. He's at New York University now. But my mother keeps up with Elaine Shipley. We lived next door to the Shipleys in Dallas. I don't know why Sally asked me to be maid of honor. Will, this traffic is impossible," she wailed. "We'll never make it to the hospital."

"Muffy'll understand. She knows what the freeway is like." *Get back to you and me.* Cecily had fallen silent. It was up to him again. "This is going to be a really big wedding." That was a good one. "As far as I can tell, everybody in Dallas will be there."

"That's what my mother told me," Cecily said. "Except she said 'the most important people in Dallas.'"

"Yep, everybody from the mayor to the Dallas Grand Opera director. Oh, and Congressman Galloway and both senators. You keep up with local politics?"

"No."

So there was no point in pursuing that tack any further. Will cleared his throat. "Where's your practice?"

It was a simple question, but it seemed to jar her a little. "Blue Hill, Vermont."

"Why Vermont?"

This time she hesitated even longer. Maybe it was just because the traffic had started to move. "It's where the big bucks are in my field."

"Yeah, you have to think about things like that." In spite of himself, he was getting interested. "You have a specialty?"

"I'm in general medicine, but…but I've gotten pretty good at high-risk deliveries."

"No kidding? What a coincidence for you to be right there in Sally's wedding party just when Muffy needed you." He considered what she'd said. "I'm surprised, though. I would have thought the big bucks would be in New York, Chicago—a big city full of career women who don't have kids until they're getting close to forty."

"Yes, but Vermont's such a beautiful place," she said, "and the pace is slower. No place is perfect, of course."

"What's the downside?"

"It gets lonely sometimes." The traffic really was moving now, not quickly but steadily, and she seemed to be concentrating on it.

"You have your patients." He gazed at her, increasingly curious about how she lived her life.

"Yes, but..."

"You don't like socializing with them?"

A corner of her mouth quirked. A tic, probably, brought on by the car that had cut so sharply in front of them it made even him nervous. "I'm very fond of my patients," she said, "but I have to admit they have certain limitations. Not big readers. Not particularly exciting to talk to. Very little interest in theater or movies or concerts. Unsophisticated tastes in food."

Damn. She was a snob. Didn't mind treating the mountain men or delivering their women's babies but looked down on them socially and intellectually. Too bad. Just looking at her, he wouldn't have thought she'd feel that way.

"What about you? What did you grow up to be?"

"A CPA. But I'm good to my mother."

She gave him an odd look. Most people, when he told them what he did, immediately told him their favorite accountant joke, which tended to illustrate the cold humorless nature of people who chose the profession. When she didn't say anything at all, he added immodestly, "I have a law degree, too. I'm with Helpern and Ridley in Houston. I'm Gus's tax man."

"Ah. But you know Sally, too?"

"Sally's my cousin."

"All in the family." She actually took her eyes off the road and gave him a smile. If she hadn't, he might have gone back to worrying about Gus's reported income.

"You can trust family," he said, hoping it was true.

"You like your work?"

He loved his work. "It's a living." He patted the

dashboard of the Audi. "Buys the toys. How about you? You like being a doctor?"

She hesitated briefly, then said, "Too much, apparently."

"Meaning?"

She sighed, then took a deep breath and seemed to be gearing up to say something important. "With no social life to speak of, I've really let myself go. Just look at my dress. And my hair. I'm a mess. I didn't realize it until I walked on to the rehearsal scene. This wedding is a fashion show!"

He didn't think she was a mess at all. She looked fresh and wholesome, and he liked it. "You look just fine to me, and I don't think patients notice what the doctor is wearing."

"Mine are more undiscriminating than most." It came out like a groan. "It doesn't bother me there, but here, with Sally and all her gorgeous bridesmaids... I mean, who'd choose me unless I..." She came to a halt. "Will," she said, "may I ask you an extremely personal question?"

He sat up a little straighter. He hoped the "extremely personal" question would turn out to be really *personal*. "Whose person?" he said. "Mine or yours?"

"Mine."

"Sure."

Her head swiveled. "What can I do to myself in the next couple of hours to make a man want to have sex with me?"

He jolted upright. His sunglasses flew off his head. The car swerved. Cecily shrieked. Will grabbed the steering wheel. He put one foot down hard on the floor of the car to keep his balance. The crunch told him that's where his sunglasses had fallen.

It was his signal to get new sunglasses.

After he'd taken this woman to bed.

NOW THAT THE CAR WAS GOING straight again and Cecily's were the only hands on the steering wheel, she had time to realize the enormity of the mistake she'd made. Earlier, when she'd had her epiphany while driving the endless highway toward the peculiarly distant hospital, she'd realized she needed help if she were to find a man to release the pressure inside her. Seeing Will again had caused the problem, but Will was married. He couldn't provide the solution.

Still, for a moment she'd let herself imagine Will as The Man, imagine him looking at her. Her clothes—limp, frumpy, with no logos anywhere. Her hair—just the way God made it, somewhere between blond and brown and tied back so she wouldn't have to look at it.

Even if he—not Will, of course, because it couldn't be Will—were undiscriminating enough, horny enough, to get to the undressing stage with her, how would he react to her severe cotton bra, her enormous white cotton panties? They weren't even snowy white. The water in Blue Hill was very hard and tended to turn white things gray.

He'd said she looked fine, but what would you expect a man to say? Truth was, she was clean—or had been that morning, which seemed like a lifetime ago—with the possible exception of her toenails and allowing for the grayness of her lingerie. It was the only positive thing she could say about herself. As for metamorphosing into the kind of woman one of the other men—not Will—would be interested in, she didn't have a clue. Eyelash batting, even with mascara added, was not enough.

It required the proper external trappings, the area in which she was most clueless, always had been. While she'd lived at home, her mother had functioned as her personal dresser, bringing home trendy outfits appropriate for every occasion, dragging her to beauty salons. She'd been thrilled to be out on her own, away from all that fussing. And look what had happened to her.

But Will fit in with these friends of Sally's, looked like them, dressed like them. He'd know. And since he was married and they weren't total strangers, she'd decided she wouldn't feel too embarrassed about consulting him. If she couldn't have him, she could pick his brains, because she wanted to look like the kind of woman Will would fall hard for—if he weren't married with a new baby. But she'd said it all wrong and she'd scared the dickens out of him.

Her face went hot with mortification. He'd thought she was asking *him* to have sex with her. He'd settled back into his seat, panting—from fear, undoubtedly—simply tossing the shards of his sunglasses from one hand to the other. Most men would have yelled at her for swerving like that. She thought he was probably too unnerved to yell.

"Sorry I jumped," he said suddenly. "You surprised me, that's all."

"I'm the one who's sorry," she said, feeling miserable. "That's another downside to being…" She'd come close to saying, "being with cows." She'd have to tell him eventually that she was a vet. When the time was right. "…being so isolated. You forget how to express yourself. I said what I said very badly."

"You didn't say it badly. It was just that—"

"You're being polite. In fact, I made you think I

was asking you to have sex with me, when nothing could have been further from my mind."

She was puzzled by his long silence, until he said, "Really."

She forged ahead. "Of course not. That would be terrible of me. What I meant was… Well, let me start at the beginning."

"Okay."

Her skin prickled when she felt his fixed gaze on her cheek. "It's just that I haven't had sex in a while. Not by choice," she added hastily. She still wasn't saying it right. She didn't want to sound sad and deprived. She wanted to sound bright and brassy, lusty and lascivious, to keep her tone breezy and confident. Most of all, she wanted to sound as if she'd planned all along to turn the wedding weekend into a sexual marathon. "What matters to me is my career. Sex is something I decided to handle with one-night stands now and then. You know, nothing serious. No strings."

"Just casual sex."

"That's me, your typical slut-puppy." *Sure I am.* "But I've hit this little snag. There aren't a lot of men available for casual sex in Blue Hill." *Like none, and if I did find someone, the whole town would be talking about it the next morning.* "So I thought this weekend would be a good time to catch up, but now that I see my competition, I can tell I don't have the—"

"The steelo to tap anybody?" He'd grown very still.

"Have the *what?*"

"Never mind. Go ahead."

"Anyway, I need to do an instant makeover, head to toe, inside and out. And since you were an old friend and married with a new baby and all that, I felt comfortable asking you where to start." She gave him a sidelong glance.

Will froze with his mouth hanging open. She thought he and Muffy were married? That he was the father of Muffy's baby? It was such a chilling thought that every atom in his body wanted to shout, *No! It's not true!*

Except for that one atom that whispered, *Maybe it's the only reason having sex with you is the furthest thing from her mind*. Because he'd felt a connection, felt a spark between them. So if he told her he wasn't married to Muffy, wasn't the father of the baby...

He couldn't tell her now. He didn't want to end this up-close-and-personal conversation. But when the right time came, he definitely wanted Cecily to know he was single. Then he'd find out if that was her only reason for rejecting him—again. Now he wanted to get to the hospital as fast as possible. As bad as her sense of direction seemed to be, she'd never figure out she was making a U-turn and going right back in the direction they'd come from. The hospital was in fact about six blocks from the church. "Start moving to the right," he said abruptly. "There's the Preston Road exit. I know a shortcut to the hospital."

"What?" Cecily yelled, then sped up and began demonically shifting lanes. Will closed his eyes, seeing his life pass before him as she shot in front of a sixteen-wheeler going eighty, honking furiously and flashing its lights. And then she had them flying down the exit ramp and coasting onto the access road without looking to see if anyone was coming.

His eyes were still closed when the car came to a stop. "Left or right on Preston Road?" Cecily said in a voice as calm as an angel's. "Will, I said left or right? Which way to the hospital? Oh, for God's sake, Will, have you fainted again?"

# 3

---

"I THOUGHT I'D LOST ALL MY hazardous driving skills," Cecily marveled, "but they came right back to me, just like riding a bicycle."

"You do excel at hazardous driving."

She shot him a glance. He hadn't fainted, apparently, but he did look stunned. "Now if only I could remember how to clean myself up, blow-dry my hair properly, do my nails, exfoliate and moisturize regularly...."

"I'm telling you, you look fine."

"I used to look fine," she corrected him. "I honestly think my mother kept me at home instead of sending me to boarding school so she could have a few more years of keeping my hair trimmed and buying my clothes, hoping it would sink in. But the minute I left home— Oh, look, Will, the hospital." Her right turn might have been a little abrupt. Will paled again. "I'm so glad we're finally here. I'm just sorry I didn't get to pick your brains a little more about specifics— you know, the clothes and underwear."

"Maybe we'll find a spare minute to discuss... clothes and underwear."

Nothing she'd love more than a spare minute with Will, but every minute that went by was more dangerous to her psyche. The sooner she was away from him, the better. She'd take a taxi back to the hotel, go to Sutherland's downtown and use her own best judgment to change from ugly duckling to swan.

She looked at him again, worrying that she'd already overstepped the bounds by talking to him about something as personal as bras and panties. "I hope I haven't embarrassed you."

"No, no, not at all. I'm...I used to be an expert in the field of sexy women."

She was glad she'd driven up an oak-lined drive and not up a tree when Will put her in the category of "sexy women." He directed her into a parking lot with Glen Oaks Care Center signs plastered all over the place. The neighborhood looked familiar, very like the one in which the St. Andrews church was located. The hospital was a pleasant-looking red-brick structure with white trim and many wings and outbuildings.

Cecily felt that the moment of truth had arrived. She couldn't lie anymore about being a veterinarian and she wanted to come clean with Will first, ask him if it would come as too great a shock to Muffy. "Will," she said, "there's something I really must tell you before we see Muffy."

He was unbuckling his seat belt, pocketing his keys, reaching for the door handle. He turned to her, curiosity in his gaze but something else, too, something compelling that drew her toward a promise he could never keep.

Her heart sank. He thought she was going to confess that he'd turned her on, that she'd hoped to lead him astray, distract him from total concentration on Muffy and the baby, and that's why she'd been talking about sex. He couldn't be more wrong.

Her confession would probably make him mad. Maybe he'd be so ugly-mad she'd never want to see him again—although Will ugly-mad wasn't something she could conjure up in her mind. Mad, maybe. But ugly? Impossible.

But she would go straight home tomorrow and never see him again and everything would be all right.

Everything except her. He'd gotten out of the car, apparently figuring she could make her confession on the run. Or maybe he wasn't all that curious after all. So she got out, too. "Will?"

"I'm listening." He was walking too fast. She lengthened her stride to match his.

"Will, I'm not a doctor."

That slowed him down. "I mean, I am a doctor, but I'm an animal doctor. A vet. It's true that I've gotten rather adept at difficult deliveries, but my difficult deliveries aren't human babies."

He paused on the ball of one foot, carefully set down his heel and moved the other foot up to match. "You're what?" To her amazement, his eyes were dancing and a smile curved his sensuous lower lip.

"I'm a veterinarian. A large-animal vet. My patients are cows and horses, sheep and pigs, your occasional goat—"

Laughter growled in his throat. "That explains why you don't date any of them."

"Yes," she said, still waiting for the ax to fall.

"Hah!" Will yelled out the word and raised his arms high above his head in a V for victory.

"See," Cecily hurried on, "that's why rural Vermont is a good place for me to be. Lots of dairy farms, horse breeding, sheep raising. That's where my big patient base is—"

"All those deliveries you bragged about were baby farm animals! Muffy's gonna trip. Wow, oh, wow, I can't wait to see her face!"

Cecily was astounded. Astounded and upset. "Will, you're treating it like a good joke on Muffy. You should be on her side. You should be mad at me for misrepresenting myself. You should be threatening litigation. You should—"

"Muffy's gonna blow a gasket," he was chanting happily. "Muffy's gonna—"

At the hospital doors he dropped his happy act and turned to her, a new man and a suddenly dangerous one. He brought his face very close to hers, apparently oblivious to the fact that the doors had opened automatically and the women at the reception desk were staring at them. "I'm going to get you for this," he said, but he smiled.

CECILY SHRANK BACK WHILE HE spoke briskly to the receptionist. "Muffy's in Twenty-Four East," he said when he came back.

"Maybe I should take a taxi home and just let you visit with her," Cecily said. Then Will could bear the burden of Muffy's rage alone.

"No, she'll want to thank you, I'm sure." Will's smile was positively evil. "Let me have a few minutes alone with her. I'll tell her about your, um, true life's work and get her calmed down, then you come up."

"If you think it's the right thing to do."

"Definitely. Hang around down here for ten minutes, then follow me up."

Right. Glumly Cecily sat down in the lobby and

thought that if she had a choice between facing an angry bull or a hysterical, hormonal woman, she'd take *el toro* any day.

"WILL! YOU'RE HERE! I'M SO glad to see you. Come look at your niece. Isn't she beautiful? You're going to be the *greatest* uncle. She'll adore you."

The woman cradling a baby in the crook of her arm and beaming at him from the hospital bed *looked* like Muffy—except for the beaming and the baby— but she didn't sound like Muffy. He was still standing in the doorway, so to make sure this was Muffy's room, he leaned back into the hall to read the number on the door and then the name on the chart. "Margaret Murchison Tidwell."

Yep, it was Muffy all right, but she'd been taken over by some alien force! Where had that sweet expression come from? That affectionate voice?

Still, those were his and Muffy's parents coming toward him, smiling as though they knew her and him both. To get in touch with reality, he strode forward to grab them in a big hug.

"Good to see you, son," his father said, sounding embarrassed.

"Does Muffy seem *changed* to you?" he muttered into his mother's ear.

"Why, no, honey, she seems like the same sweetheart she's always been," his mother murmured back. "I knew she'd make a wonderful mother. Just as you'll make a wonderful father someday."

Will looked back at Muffy with narrowed eyes. He didn't buy her new attitude for a minute. He did need her help, though.

He walked over to the bed and bent down to look

at his niece. He had to admit it, this was one cute baby. He could actually feel himself swelling with pride, imagining himself taking her to the zoo, teaching her to ride a bike….

But that would come later. He had issues now. "Gator's not here yet?"

"No." Muffy smiled softly. "He calls every five minutes, though. He's on his way from Love Field right now."

"So he'll be here any minute," Will said brightly, raising his voice.

"Well…"

"Any minute," Will said, and frowned at her. "Maybe Mom and Dad should go out and wait for him, bring him right up to the room. You know Gator. He'll be so excited, he might get lost. He'd appreciate a welcoming committee."

She raised an eyebrow and contemplated Will for a long, scary moment. "Oh, yes, I know he would. Mom, Daddy, would you go outside and wait for Gator? He can't be more than a couple of minutes away."

"Gator's parents will be along pretty soon, too, I imagine," Will said, knowing perfectly well they'd have to drive up from Waco, a good hour and a half from the hospital.

"And," Muffy added, "I really need some body lotion from the gift shop. I forgot mine."

The idea of body lotion seemed to pull their mother's trigger. "Of course, darling," Mrs. Murchison said warmly. "Nothing more important than body lotion right now. We don't want stretch marks. I hope they have something nice. Come on, Bill, let's look out for Gator and his parents. Back soon, angels."

"What are you up to?" Muffy whispered when their parents were out the door.

"The doctor," Will said tersely. "I know her. I've had the hots for her since I was at Exeter. But she got the idea you and I are married."

"Oh, my God," Muffy said, sounding much more like the old Muffy.

"I want to keep it that way for a while."

"Why would you want to do that?"

Why? Because he'd just realized that as long as Cecily thought he was safely married, she'd let him advise her about sexy clothes and lingerie. He might even be able to con her into letting him come shopping with her.

The idea really turned him on.

He cleared his throat. "I have my reasons. You'll go along, right?"

Muffy gave her little daughter a lingering, loving glance. "I do have other, more important things going on in my own life right now," she began, then looked up at Will. "But twins have a sacred trust to lie for each other." She sighed.

"I sure kept you out of a hell of a lot of trouble," Will said and took another look at the baby. She was a doll. Now was the time to put Muffy through the acid test, find out how far her unprecedented loving mood stretched. "Incidentally, Muff, Cecily's actually a—"

But the door opened and Cecily's head poked tentatively into the room.

IN THE LOBBY, CECILY HAD KEPT one eye on her watch and the other on the steady stream of visitors, home-bound patients and medical personnel who flowed through the lobby. Friday must be a popular dismissal day. At last her ten minutes were up and she started for the elevator. When the doors opened, an attractive older couple stepped out. Cecily did a double take.

The woman was slim and pretty, her hair a pale shade of blonde that suggested dark hair gone gray. The man, though, was a dead ringer for Will, or the way Will would look twenty-five or thirty years from now. Either these were Will's parents or Muffy was one of those women who'd married her father. She thought about coming right out and asking them, but considered the complications if she introduced herself as "the doctor who delivered the baby." So she merely smiled, went up to Twenty-Four East and shyly stuck her head through the doorway.

"Oh, look, Will, it's the doctor!" Muffy said. "You're so sweet to come and check on me."

Cecily stumbled forward, feeling stunned. Was this the same Muffy? Everything she'd told Will at the delivery scene, those things about women not being themselves during labor, had been true. There was nothing terrible about Muffy. She'd merely been having a baby.

Muffy grabbed Cecily's hand. "You were great," she said. Her voice was warm and soft. "I can't thank you enough."

"She did a good job, didn't she?" Will said, his tone nearly as warm and soft as Muffy's, but his voice did different things to Cecily than Muffy's did. "Wasn't it amazing, finding a top-notch doctor in the wedding party? You know what she told me in the car, Muff? She says she's an expert in difficult deliveries!"

Cecily was startled. He was supposed to have told Muffy already that she was a vet.

"No kidding," Muffy said, looking wide-eyed. "What a coincidence! Gosh," she said, looking positively saintly, "I must have a guardian angel."

Cecily saw the look Will gave Muffy—a slanty-eyed, teasing glance—before he said, "She's an expert, all right, an expert at delivering calves, colts and piglets, not babies." He crossed his arms over his chest. "Your guardian angel sent you a *vet*. How about that, Muff?"

Cecily felt the tension in the air. Something was going on between Will and Muffy that had nothing to do with her or with her being a vet. Her stomach tightened.

Muffy stared wide-eyed at her for a moment, then at Will. Her face suddenly lit up in a gleeful smile. "That's the funniest thing I ever heard." She began laughing.

Will looked dumbfounded. "My God, she's for real," he murmured.

"What?" Muffy and Cecily said in unison.

"Uh, nothing, nothing. Come here, Cecily, and take a look at this baby."

Cecily took a look, feeling her heart melt at the sight of the tiny hands, the long lashes, the wispy dark curls, the button nose. "She's adorable," she said. "She's going to make you two so happy." Will couldn't be having any problems with this sweet, motherly version of Muffy, couldn't be thinking about divorce. And he couldn't under any circumstances be thinking of giving up this beautiful baby. Cecily was trying really hard to feel happy for both of them.

Muffy gave Will a smile that might even be called sappy. "We haven't decided on a name yet, *darling*, but now I think I'd like to name her Cecily. Cecily," Muffy said to the baby, "meet Cecily Connaught, the miracle woman who brought you into the world under the most terrible conditions—"

"Well, no," Cecily interrupted, made intensely nervous by the conversation and the thought of Will having a baby Cecily. "Not all dairy farmers keep their barns in—oof!" Will had grabbed her in such a strenuous hug that it took the breath out of her.

"We sure will," he said heartily. "We'll name her Cecily. Maybe," he continued as he released Cecily to give her a soulful look, "you would be her godmother."

"Oh, yes," Muffy cried. "It would mean so much to us."

"I'm flattered," Cecily said, her nervousness reaching the panic level, "but I—"

"Thank you," Will and Muffy said together, giving her oddly similar grateful glances.

The telephone rang and Muffy reached for it. "Just a second," she said, and put her hand over the mouthpiece. "It's our friend Gator," she said to Will.

"You talk to him," Will said. "I'll take Cecily home and be back as soon as possible, *sweetheart*."

"Absolutely not," Cecily said. She'd never felt as firm about anything in her life. She couldn't stand another second in the confines of a car with Will. "I'll call a taxi."

"No way!" Muffy said with a quick glance at Will. "What kind of manners would that be? I insist that Will take you back to the hotel." She went back briefly to the phone. "Hang on, Gator. We're having a little argument here." She smiled. "I know. What else is new?"

Cecily felt confused. Maybe they did argue a lot. Maybe Muffy was just being polite because Cecily was there. She stamped on the thought. She still couldn't have Will. Period.

"One more thing," Will said. "I need to buy cigars and Cecily needs to do a little shopping, and when I take Cecily to the hotel, I'll go ahead and register. You won't mind if I'm not back for a couple of hours."

Now Cecily was having a full anxiety attack. "No, you don't need to take me shopping—"

"Take all the time you need, darling. Mom and Daddy will be along soon."

"And my mom and dad."

"Right. Your mom and dad, too."

Maybe that was the source of the tension, their parents.

"So we'll say goodbye." Will stepped up to the bed and gave Muffy a peck on the cheek, then leaned way down to give the child—who was apparently going to be baby Cecily—a soft, gentle kiss. "You and I are going to be best friends," he whispered.

A tiny finger gripped his, and something intense gripped Cecily's heart. She stepped up, too. "And I'm your godmother Cecily," she said, wondering how the hell she was going to be a decent godmother to Will's baby.

"A godmother who will reappear at just the moment you need her," Will said in a surprisingly commanding voice, "but for now is going to disappear."

"Gator," Cecily heard Muffy say, "When will you get here?" Then she yelled, "Will! Can you talk to Gator?"

Will put his head back through the door just long enough to say, "He just wants to remind me to buy cigars. Tell him I'll get them on this trip."

"I just said I'd be that precious baby's godmother," Cecily said as Will dragged her down the hall with surprising speed.

"Very kind of you."

"But we hardly know each other, and I'll be in Vermont while little Cecily's in Houston with you. Feel free to change your mind. Minds. I know Muffy's a little overemotional right now."

Will's step slowed. "She's transformed."

"Transformed?"

"Yes." He frowned deeply. "Having that baby did something to her body chemistry."

"Whatever," Cecily said. "Now you two can truly bond with each other and little Cecily."

"Believe me," Will said, "we're bonded."

"Well, good." For him anyway, and for Muffy and the other Cecily. As for this Cecily, she needed to be out of his atmosphere and fast. "You really are very nice to take me back to the hotel," she said, "but we're not going to waste any time shopping. I'll go to Sutherland's. It's just a block or so from the Courtland."

"That's right, it is."

"So you'll take me right back to the hotel?"

"If that's what you want."

It wasn't what she wanted, but it was the only alternative she could bear. The tigress, she feared, had lost her appetite for anyone but Will.

No. She couldn't let that happen. She had to remember that her persona for the next twenty-four hours was that of a skanky ho, to whom a one-night stand was as natural as delivering a baby.

WILL COULDN'T STOP MARVELING at the change in Muffy. They'd just coordinated a successful team effort to keep Cecily in the dark about his marital status. There were too many fingers on his right hand to count the number of times in their tumultuous past he and Muffy had coordinated on anything except keeping her out of trouble.

Now all he had to do was get Cecily's mind going in the direction of having sex with him and this could turn out to be one of the greatest days of his life.

"Before you go shopping, we should talk," he said. "You'd asked me about clothes." He was driving now, to his relief, and Cecily hadn't protested.

"Oh. Yes. It's not that I don't know how to be seductive," she said, and catching her slanted look, all Will could do was silently agree with her statement. "It's just that I'm out of practice. I didn't notice any of the groomsmen giving me a second glance, and a groomsman would be so…convenient. What should I wear to signal that I'm available? Um, I mean hot and horny and ready for action." She cleared her throat.

The expression jarred Will and it upset him unaccountably to hear that she was thinking about the rest of the groomsmen, though he was grateful that three of them were married and Chaz, the megajock in running clothes, was gay.

The one person he didn't know was the best man. It was odd, come to think of it, that all Gus's attendants were Sally's friends except the best man, who was an unknown just as Gus was. Will had met him at a couple of parties, and he hadn't been with a woman. It was possible he was single.

He'd have to be watched.

And so would Gus—for different reasons. The little hum of alarm that often hit him when he thought about the mysterious Gus returned in full force.

But Cecily was waiting for an answer about a…a dress. He was supposed to describe a sexy dress.

"Oh, something short," he said, slicing his hand across his legs just above the knee. "And black and low here," he said, making a big scoop on his chest. He thought about scooping that line along the tops of Cecily's breasts, and feeling a familiar heat in his groin, shifted beneath the steering wheel.

"I figured you'd suggest something like that." She paused, gazed at him. "You sure you feel like driving?"

"Positive," Will said.

"What about underwear?"

*Mine are getting tight.* "What about it?"

"What kind of underwear do men like?"

"Well, some like briefs but others prefer boxers." He wished he were in boxers right now.

She gave him a look. "*Women's* underwear. What kind do men like to see on *women?*"

This really got his juices going. "Uh," he said eloquently, shoving his butt back against the seat and leaning over the steering wheel, still trying to get comfortable. "Well…"

"Is it true that peekaboo lingerie actually turns a man on more than nakedness?" she persisted.

He realized she had no idea he was mentally holding a slinky nightie to her shoulders as if she were a paper doll. He had to get on the program here, had to act like a married man giving sage, *platonic* advice. He leaned back again and began, "Okay, here's what men like to see women wear." And then he actually started thinking about it.

"I don't know what other men like because guys are more apt to sit around talking about women's boobs than about their clothes, so I'll just tell you what I like. When I pick—" he caught himself just in time "—when I used to pick up a woman for a date, I wanted her to look like she cared about me, not what other women thought about her clothes. I wanted her to look pretty. Soft. Nice. Kind. Glad to see me."

Cecily was giving him her full attention as he delivered this sentiment he'd never expressed before, not even to himself. It embarrassed him to realize he'd revealed something so personal about himself. He glanced at her quickly to see how she'd taken it and saw sadness on her face.

It worried him. "You okay? Was it something I said?"

Her face cleared up. "No. I'm fine."

He couldn't help hoping that what had made her sad was thinking he was married to Muffy. Should he confess right now that he was single, available and as hot and horny as she could ever imagine being?

What if she'd really meant it when she said she didn't want to have sex with him? If it had nothing to do with her thinking he was married? He wasn't ready for that big a disappointment. The more time he spent with her—and the longer he kept her away from single men in the wedding party—the better his chances with her.

He was taking her shopping whether she liked it or not. He wondered how she'd look in a thong.

His mouth watered just thinking about it.

# 4

---

THE COURTLAND WAS A DOWNTOWN HOTEL, old, elegant and a Dallas tradition of beauty, comfort and exquisite service. Early oil millionaires had stayed there, stomping across the marble floors and Aubusson rugs in their dusty boots, heading for the dark-paneled bar and a bourbon and branch. Will pulled up in front of the hotel, wrestled Cecily's medical bag away from her and handed it and his own bag to the porter, then asked for valet parking. "We'll shop now and check in later," he said.

"No!" Cecily said, literally feeling frightened. "*I'm* shopping. *You're* going back to the hospital."

"I have to buy cigars."

"They sell cigars at Sutherland's?"

"I'm sure they do."

"Then you shop for cigars, and I'll shop for clothes. You were very helpful in the car."

"I'll be even more helpful in the store. We really didn't get into specifics about the underwear. Besides, I can show you easier than I can tell you."

"I think that would make me feel very uncomfortable." Not think, *know*. And she was already about as uncomfortable as she could stand.

"But why?" He couldn't have looked more innocent. "We're old friends. You've met Muffy. You heard Muffy say we should take as long as we needed to do your shopping. I'm only here to help you make the right choices and wow the guys."

"Well, I—" He really wasn't giving her another option. His hand gripped her elbow as he hustled her across the street, down the sidewalk and through the old-fashioned front doors of the store, then sped her past the handbags and cosmetics and onto the escalator.

"We'll try the third floor," he said.

Several minutes later, Cecily was thumbing through a rack of black cocktail dresses. This part wasn't too difficult. *Just pick one. The sexiest one.* "How about this?" she said, trying for a confident, tigress sort of tone. Just looking at it made perspiration pop out on her upper lip. Not from arousal. From fear. She'd rather treat a shark with a toothache than walk out the door in a two-and-a-half-foot length of silk jersey with spaghetti straps.

But if Sutherland's was selling it, Dallas was wearing it. Will didn't seem all that excited about it. "Wow," he said, his lips tight, thin line. "Wear that to the rehearsal dinner tonight and men will be lining up outside your room afterward. Which is the point, I guess."

No, that was going a little far. One man would be quite enough, if he was the right man. She darted a look at him, but he was still staring at the dress, so she grabbed the price tag and stared at it instead. "My God. I could make it myself with a piece of cloth and a staple gun. Explain to me why it's worth seven hundred dollars."

"Ours is not to reason why," Will said.

"But just to buy."

"Right." He folded his arms over his chest. "Wrong. It's overpriced."

"Money is no object." She slung the dress over her arm, indicating her intention to flee.

"So your practice pays well."

"Pretty well, and I don't spend a third of what I make." She shifted from one foot to the other, feeling like a kid who had to go to the bathroom, which was not her problem. Her problem was suddenly imagining Will seeing her in the dress, not out in public but in the privacy of a shared room, and the image had started her hormones flowing.

"Why?"

Damn, he was persistent. "Nowhere to spend it. Nothing to spend it on. But don't worry. I've got it all locked up in mutual funds. Look, Will, you're supposed to be buying the cigars, and I'm supposed to be buying the clothes. We don't have time for a lecture on estate planning."

"Right, right."

But did he say goodbye and leave? No.

"I still think you should do a little more looking. That dress, well, it *is* sort of…obvious." He was getting a stubborn, alpha expression on his face.

"No time to look."

"Guys scare easy," Will argued. "I'd suggest something more subtle."

She was feeling like a stubborn alpha herself. "Will, I don't need the kind of guy who gets scared by a dress. I have no time for subtlety. Obvious is what I'm after. I'm trying it on. Thanks for your help. 'Bye, and good luck finding cigars."

"But—" was the last thing she heard him say before she fled to the fitting room.

WILL HAD A FEELING HE WAS IN over his head. If he'd told her the truth, they might be lying together in a nice, soft bed right now and she wouldn't be planning to go out that night looking like a hooker. He really didn't want her to. The more he thought about it, the surer he was that Derek Stafford, the best man, was single. He was positive the man would be at the rehearsal dinner—the best man always gave a speech, didn't he? And Stafford looked like a wolf. He didn't want Cecily shaking her booty in front of any wolves.

Okay, no more getting scared. Forget the cigars. Let Gator buy his own. Will would go in search of the lingerie department so he could steer Cecily right to it before she had a chance to argue with him, and on the way…

He halted, staring at a mannequin. There it was—The Dress. It was a thin silk dress, sleeveless, just the color of Cecily's skin, with a faded-looking design of flowers that were blue like Cecily's eyes. A soft, floppy ruffle ran over one shoulder and down the front to the hem, where it went around and came up again underneath. How was a mystery, but it made the skirt open up in the front in a flirty sort of way.

It was just a soft, sweet, pale, pretty—he glanced at the price tag—*expensive* little dress, but something about it got his attention, just the way Cecily did. She might look soft and sweet, but the force of her personality reached out and grabbed him in an assertive way that knocked him off his feet.

She'd been like that with the horses at the stable—sweet, loving and firm as an orthopedic bed. Thinking about beds made him wonder if she'd be an assertive lover. He began imagining her in the dress, wearing it to have dinner with him, just the two of them at a small table in his room. No, her room—it was probably neater. She'd sit down at the table, then she'd cross her legs ever so slowly, and the dress would part in the front....

At last he'd see her legs. He couldn't wait. Until today, he'd never seen her in anything but jodhpurs and long-sleeved shirts. Today he'd glimpsed her slim, well-toned arms and her ankles, and they were pale and slim. All he could see of her was pale and slim, so she must be pale and slim all over—her calves, her thighs....

The dress, imagining Cecily in it, imagining her long, pale, slim thighs wrapped around him, was making him feel hot and jangly all over. He summoned a salesperson and demanded the dress in the same size he'd noticed on the tag hanging from the black dress Cecily had picked out, then raced back toward the fitting room he'd seen her vanish into.

A salesperson tackled him. "May I help you?"

"No, thanks. I'm looking for the woman in the flowered dress—"

"With the white satin stilettos?"

"That would be the one. She's trying on a dress." He took off.

"Wait, sir, you can't go in there...."

Yes, he could. He was already there. "Cecily," he yelled into the long bank of stalls. "Where are you?"

He listened to little shrieks from other stalls before Cecily's calm voice said, "You're not supposed to be in here, Will. You're supposed to be buying cigars." She stepped through one of the doors. "But since you're here, what do you think? I think I look like a billboard advertising sex."

A tsunami of desire swept through him. That was

exactly what she looked like—a billboard advertising sex. The dress skimmed over soft curves without hiding anything. She'd taken off her bra to try on the dress, and tight little nipples showed through the thin silk, as did the shadow of her belly button. The fabric outlined her thighs so suggestively that again he imagined them wrapped around him, the dress riding up to her waist....

Was he scared? No. Just scared to let anybody else see her in that dress. And scared to realize how much he didn't want anybody else to see her in that dress. Why should he care? What did it matter, really, in the long run?

But somehow it did. He raised his fist and shouted, "Take it off!" This simple, straightforward request seemed to set off a chain reaction in the dressing room, because the noise level shot way up.

Cecily stared at him. "Will, have you lost your mind? If I'd suspected you'd turn into a lecher, I wouldn't have asked you for help in the first place."

He realized why he couldn't make himself clear to her—he was too aroused to be coherent. "Take that dress off before anybody else sees you in it," he insisted, "and put this one on." It seemed a reasonable enough thing to ask. What was everybody getting so excited about?

At last, Cecily focused her monitor-screen-blue eyes on the dress he'd brought back with him. This was good because it meant she'd finally realized he wasn't acting like a jerk in a strip joint with his "Take it off!" It was bad because he'd figured out he really liked having them focused on him, even if it did make him dizzy.

"Oh," she said, and her voice sounded soft and

surprised. "It's so pretty. But Will," she continued, and to his disappointment, her voice firmed up, "pretty isn't what we're after. I want to look like a large-animal trap."

"What are they talking about? Animal traps?" A querulous voice came from a stall in the fitting-room area.

"Sounded like it. Lock your door, Mama."

"Try it on," Will said, ignoring the voices. "One man's animal trap is another man's turnoff. You never know."

She gave him an odd look, but she disappeared inside the stall. "I'll wait," he called out to her.

"I'm afraid not, sir," said the security guard who stepped up beside him.

Oops. He'd been busted.

Will was big, but the security officer was bigger. Will was tough, but the security officer looked as if he could take down the entire defensive line of the Dallas Cowboys single-handedly. In the absence of superior strength, skilled diplomacy was called for.

"Officer, I can explain," he said. "I expressed myself badly. My only purpose in being here—"

"Quiet down, buddy, and come along with me. We can do this nice and polite or—"

"Daphne, are you sure this is the women's dressing room?" It was the querulous voice again. "It seems to be full of men."

"It's okay, Mama. That's the police. They'll be out of here in a minute."

"Officer," Cecily said breathlessly from behind her door, "please don't arrest him. We have a situation here."

Will let out a grateful breath. The officer put his

hands on his hips and glared, looking like a guy who'd heard everything by now and was anticipating another whopper.

"We had to do a little shopping for me in a big hurry because he has to get back to the hospital to his wife and new baby. He's only here to buy cigars, but I needed a little help picking out a dress, so— Oh! This feels *so good*."

Her voice had been coming and going as she reasoned with the security man. Will could have guessed when the dress went over her head, when she wriggled it down over her hips, when she angled her arms around to reach the zipper, when she felt the silk slithering against her skin.

If the security officer noticed his erection, Will would find himself in prison for life. Swiftly he shut out the image of Cecily combined with slithering silk.

The officer had indeed tensed up again. "Doesn't make much sense," he said, but he seemed to be weakening a little at the cries of "A new daddy!" "How sweet!" "Congratulations, Daddy" that were coming from stalls up and down the length of the dressing room.

"No, it doesn't make much sense," Cecily said. She sounded dreamy now, and Will was forced into another fight against his testosterone level. "That's what I'm telling you. We have a situation. Okay, I'm taking this dress. It's a—" her voice faltered a little "—twelve-hundred-dollar dress." It grew stronger. "You want Sutherland's to make this sale, don't you? If you take Will away, I'll have to focus on finding him a lawyer. I wouldn't dream of doing anything as trivial as buying a dress. But if you'll release him into my custody, I promise he won't get into any more trouble."

There was a whooshing sound, which meant she was taking off the dress. "Does Sutherland's have a cigar department? Because Will needs some *really good* ones, don't you, Will?" Another whoosh, and Will could almost see the flowered sundress she'd been wearing earlier settling down over her body.

"The Humidor, behind gentlemen's loungewear," said the querulous voice. "They have a small but *very special* selection. Harold always went there while I shopped."

"Now, Mama, don't start grievin'."

"I'm not grieving. I'm getting mad at him all over again. The money he burned on cigars. Enough to put me in sable instead of mink."

Will couldn't imagine how much cigars would cost at Sutherland's. Not that Sutherland's would charge more, just that they would stock nothing but the best. He saw his savings slipping away, saw himself selling stocks and bonds, dipping into his 401K. Gator would want to pay him back, but he'd pay for them himself rather than bring it up with Gator, who was one of those thrifty rich guys. Then he saw Cecily slipping out of the dressing room, the dress over her arm, her heavy, honey-blond hair escaping from its ponytail to make wisps around her face, her blue eyes sparkling with fighting spirit and he thought, *What the hell.* It was worth it.

The officer took one look at her and crumpled like a toasted marshmallow. "Is it always this exciting being around you?" she asked Will as they stepped away from the fitting room.

Will smiled. "Yes," he said, thinking things were going really well.

"No wonder Muffy gets a bit testy at times," she grumbled. "Well, thanks and goodbye again—"

"You owe me," Will said swiftly. "I helped you with clothes. You have to help me with cigars."

"Will!" She glared at him and looked like a woman who'd like to stamp her foot. Then she just flung her arms out in a gesture of defeat. "Why am I arguing? Give me a minute to pay for the dress." She began muttering to herself. "This dress costs more than I've spent on clothes in the last three years, *including* parkas and mittens and barn boots and balaclavas and sock liners." But seconds later she was engaged in complex negotiations with the salesperson. By the time she'd finished, she had the woman's promise that appropriate size-seven-narrow shoes and a small, dressy bag would be waiting with the dress thirty minutes from now, and she'd pay for the whole package when she left the store.

"Okay, now the cigars," she said. "It's really silly for me to be going with you, because what I know about cigars you could put on the tip of a cigarette, but if you truly feel I owe you…"

"I do," Will said. "I faced arrest and professional ruin to find you that dress," he said while steering her onto an escalator going up.

"Where's The Humidor?"

"You heard the lady. Behind gentlemen's lounge-wear."

"Which is?"

"Behind ladies' lingerie, I'm sure," Will lied. "That's the logical conclusion, and here we are in ladies' lingerie. What a coincidence," he marveled. "Didn't you want my advice on lingerie?"

Yes, she had mentioned wanting his advice on lingerie and she deeply regretted it. She was already in deep internal trouble. Will had unwittingly picked out a seductress of a dress, the kind that seduced the wearer as well as the viewer. The silk moving over her had felt like the caress of fingertips, making her moist and heavy between her thighs, and she'd thought about a man—not Will, of course, because he was married—but *some* man—putting his arms around her and sliding that silk against her bare breasts, her buttocks. In short, she was already wasted. The last thing she needed was to see Will fingering the lace at the waistband of a pair of cream-colored panties and eyeing her speculatively.

# 5

"I LIKE THESE PANTIES," WILL said, looking thoughtful. "I'll tell you some basic things to look for in a pair of panties. First of all, this lace isn't scratchy." He smoothed the front of the panties with his hand and her knees buckled. "How panties feel is just as important as how they look, because you know men— they like to touch. Second, these panties leave something to the imagination. Guys don't have a whole lot of imagination, but all they have is focused on women, and there they let their imaginations run wild." He spoke slowly and he sounded dreamy, as if his own imagination was already running wild. He turned the panties over. "See, they're cut low, but they'll still cover, well, almost cover… You don't mind my talking so frankly, do you?" he asked interrupting himself. He gave her an earnest look. "It's just technical stuff, really."

"Rules one and two," Cecily said briskly, her hands closing on the edge of the display table for support. "Not scratchy, not too revealing. Very helpful. Thank you." If he said the word *panties* again, particularly if he said it the way he'd been saying it, like an addict saying *chocolate*, she'd come right here in the store.

Will held up the panties. "These are all you'll need under that dress."

"No bra?" She squeaked the words.

His voice had thickened to maple syrup. "You don't need one. Just these. And bare legs. Or the stockings that just come up to the thighs."

"With lace at the top." Now she'd resorted to moaning.

"If you insist on stockings at all. Men like to grab the lace and sliiide—" he stretched out the word "—the stockings down one at a time. It's a real turn-on."

"Maybe no stockings." Her fingers shaking, Cecily found the panties in her size and moved on. "What about this?" She showed him a pale apricot camisole and matching French pants with lace trim. The outfit looked...sweet. She needed sweet right now, needed to get away from sexy quick as a bunny.

"Very nice." He cocked his head to one side and contemplated the outfit. "The camisole lets a woman's breasts go free, shows the nipples."

*Ah-h-h-h.*

"Panties like these are good, too. Lots of room in the legs for a man to run his fingers up—"

He'd said the word again. Cecily grabbed the ensemble. "Fine. Let's go."

"You're getting the idea," he said admiringly. "See, while that set just looks pretty and feminine, it's actually sexier than the more revealing stuff because the woman's body is freer inside it, so the man is more aware of the motion of her—"

"Right. I'll find a sales—"

"And in that color, you'll look nearly naked."

"—person." Cecily wiped sweat off her forehead and was on the run when he caught her by one elbow.

"On the other hand, this has its own kind of sexiness."

Uneasily, Cecily looked back. He was holding a bra, studying it intensely.

He dropped his grip on her elbow. "The way the front of this bra dips down to here, where it opens, is really sexy. And the fastener's good, too. No hooks, nothing hard or sharp, just this plastic thing that slides in and out, in and out, in and out..." He demonstrated. Repeatedly.

She snatched the bra away from him. "Get me three of these," she said, "in different colors."

"Size?"

She sent him a withering glance. "I take it back. I'll find them."

"Panties to match?"

She gritted her teeth. "Panties to match." Gritting wasn't enough. She ground her teeth and then said, "Size five."

"We shouldn't forget thongs."

"Why not?"

"Because a thong's sort of basic to the whole idea of looking sexy, isn't it?" he said. "I'll look for thongs." He wandered away. She bent over, her head to her knees, hoping it would help her start breathing again.

"I like this outfit," he called to her much too soon and in a louder voice than she would have wished. She straightened up, spotted him and rushed over just to keep him from yelling again. He was holding a black lace thong by the crotch—or what would have been the crotch if it had had enough crotch to warrant calling it one. At the same time, he was gazing at a mannequin, just a torso in a tiny, baby-blue bra of sheer lace with bikini panties to match. He turned to face her. "There's something really different about this. Don't know what it is, but I like it. Better see if it's scratchy." He ran his hand over one mannequin breast. "Nope, not scratchy."

The lace was unlined. Everything would show through it.

"Maybe it's because your eyes are that same blue. On you they'll look, you know, subtle, but wow." His voice dropped a full octave.

"Wow, huh?" Cecily could hardly breathe.

"Yeah."

"Okay." A salesperson hovered, but something about them made her back away as if she were intruding.

"Where— Here they are." She picked up a set. Her legs were trembling now. She felt as if the lower half of her body weighed a thousand pounds as she tried once again to escape to the safety of that salesperson and the closest cash register.

"You'll need something to sleep in." Will handed her the thong he was still holding and gave her a long, slow smile. "Or not sleep in."

"Something like this, I suppose." She brandished a teddy, black, trimmed with lace and red bows.

Will slouched toward the night wear. "I know men are supposed to be turned on by teddies, but personally I like something with a little more freedom. You know, the teddy has to be unsnapped or unzipped or unbuttoned, maybe it's Velcro, I don't know. Kind of spoils the—"

This time Cecily forced herself to stifle the moan. "So what do you as a man prefer, because there must be many other men who feel the same way you—"

"Nothing," Will said. "Nothing is best."

"Good," Cecily said briskly. "Look at the money I've saved. I'm all finished now, so I'll pay and we'll get on to the cigars."

"But…" Will grabbed her again. "Nothing comes later. First you have to *get* to the part where nothing is best." His voice rose slightly. "That's what you asked me, remember? How you could make the man in question want to strip off everything you're—"

"That isn't what I said!"

"It's what you meant." He gave her a serious, psychiatrist-like look of understanding.

Cecily did a little more damage to the enamel of her teeth. "You've grasped the general idea." She was getting pretty damned tired of his reminding her that this surrealistic scene was all her fault. With one simple little question she'd kidnapped a man who should have been buying cigars and cooing over his new daughter, forcing him instead into consulting with her on the matter of provocative feminine attire.

But at this point, who was forcing whom? If she'd said *cigars* once, she'd said it more times than Will had said *panties*, yet here they were in lingerie, the most dangerous place she could possibly be with Will. Of course, he was an accountant. He saw life as a matrix of horizontal and vertical columns. Once he'd started filling in a column with data related to her question—how to look desirable to a man—everything else would fly out of his head until he'd filled out the column and totaled it up. But when the "everything else" included a wife and new baby, that's when it got surreal.

How could he possibly be here with her, saying

these provocative things to her, if he loved Muffy enough to marry her and give her a child?

His voice had gone all deep and rumbly again. "I like to see a woman in something...accessible, something that says, 'Here I am. Take me.'"

"Here I am. Take me," Cecily repeated in a whisper. She couldn't help herself. Her conscience was yelling at her, but Will's voice was having a stronger effect on her.

"Yes." His gaze melted into hers. The gold in his hazel eyes glittered.

Irresistibly drawn toward the idea of starting her own personal gold rush, she leaned toward him, stepped back, leaned again—then heard a warning bell from deep in her mind. "Show me an example," she croaked.

He cleared his throat, sent all that glittering gold in another direction, looking, apparently, for examples. Cecily felt relieved and bereft at the same time.

"May I help you?"

They both whirled, Cecily feeling as guilty as a child caught misbehaving. But Will lavished a smile on the salesperson who'd appeared at his elbow and was eyeing the pile of wispy lingerie draped over Cecily's arm. "I'm looking for one of those short gown-and-robe combinations."

"It's for his wife," Cecily improvised, scurrying along behind the two of them as the saleswoman led the way. "She just had a baby, and—"

A thought struck her in midsentence. It was Muffy Will had been thinking about as they'd cruised through the lingerie. The birth of their daughter had changed Muffy from shrew to seductress. Thoughts of the new Muffy had brought the glitter to his eyes, not a dangerous attraction to Cecily. She'd heard that couples were encouraged not to make love in the last weeks of the pregnancy and couldn't for another six weeks after. Will was merely sex-starved, not contemplating infidelity.

Or was he? What if Will resented having six more long, loveless weeks ahead of him? Did he see her as his ticket to a little no-strings sex?

She would never allow Will to be unfaithful to Muffy with her. She'd never get that desperate.

Just close to that desperate.

She turned her back on Will and the saleswoman, afraid the woman would take one good look at her face and know she was a good-for-nothing liar. Across the room she saw a familiar face, one she couldn't quite place. He was in the section politely referred to as Sexy Plus, ducking around a rack of gown-and-negligee sets suitable for the bigger woman.

"Oh, look, there's Congressman Galloway," the saleswoman said.

Bingo! "Shouldn't you go over and speak to him, Will?" Anything to get him away from shorty gowns.

"Oh, yes, do," burbled the salesperson. "He must be buying something pretty for his wife." She paused. "She's a skinny little thing, though. I'd better help him find the right size. Women get real mad when their husbands bring home things that are too big."

"Right," Will said briskly. "You can help him right after you help me. I'm looking for a sheer, *very* sheer—"

"You should introduce yourself and tell him you have a new baby," Cecily insisted, the words *very sheer*, shaking her up even more than *panties*. "Politicians love to be recognized. He'll probably issue a proclamation declaring it Cecily Murchison Day. It will be a memento she'll cherish forever."

"I'm not a groupie," Will said in a voice that didn't invite her to go on babbling. "Let the poor guy shop in peace."

"In peace, but in Sexy Plus" the saleswoman said pointedly, "when he should be in Petites."

"As I said," Will said, his voice rising a little, "after we find this very sheer…"

While Will selected something the salesperson showed him, Cecily gave in to total despair. She'd never in her life felt so turned on, so obsessed by desire, but she was starting to feel certain she wouldn't find a man to relieve her need. Without even turning around, she fished out her credit card and held it out behind her. "Whatever he picks out," she said over her shoulder to the saleswoman, "it's my baby gift to the happy couple." She looked down at the panties and bras dangling over her arm. "These are for me." She held them out behind her, too, and felt them being taken from her cold, dead fingers.

In the last few minutes, a terrible truth had become crystal clear to her. It didn't matter how attractive she made herself to the available men who might appear on the wedding scene. The only man she could possibly have sex with this weekend was standing behind her, chatting happily with the salesperson about the joys of parenthood and the treatment of colic.

She couldn't have him, even though she felt hotter, needier, readier than ever before in her life. So what was she going to do about it?

Help him buy cigars. And maybe he'd give her one. A cigar sounded really sexy right now.

"Wow, these cigars smell good."

"Feel free to smoke one as soon as we leave the store."

"Can't afford to. I'm hanging on to a thousand dollars' worth of something that will eventually go up in smoke. Why couldn't Muffy's friends just get together and set fire to a thousand-dollar bill?"

"My dress cost more than that. And the shoes! Four hundred for a spike heel and a strap across the toe?" She sounded tense and nervous.

"Four hundred for those little words *Jimmy Choo* nobody will ever see because you'll be standing on them."

"She did a nice job picking out those two skirts and tops, though," Cecily said. "Nice for Sutherland's, anyway. How was I to know those little skirts cost so much? And whoever heard of a cotton T-shirt costing two hundred dollars? Sally's friends must all be gazillionaires."

Will realized he should have said earlier, "our friends," not "Muffy's friends." He couldn't keep up the game of being Muffy's husband a minute longer. The lingerie shopping had been the last straw.

He hadn't made up the thing about men's imaginations being focused on women. Imagining those little pieces of silk and lace on Cecily had sent his testosterone sky-high, and he was pretty sure he was getting signals from her that she'd be amenable to reducing his hormone levels if only he weren't a married man. He was dying to tell her he was single, available and hotter than a car seat in July, then whiz back to the hotel with all due speed to watch her model her new underwear.

So where could he tell her and how? He chewed

his lip. It was important to tell her before they checked into the hotel.

"Would you mind a quick trip up the elevator to the infants' department?" he improvised. "Muffy's not happy with little Cecily's diaper bag. You might do a better job of picking out one she'd like."

The expression on her face filled him with hope. He was pretty sure that the last thing in the world she wanted to do was help him buy a diaper bag.

But she was nice enough to agree. In fact, there was something despairing about the way she agreed, her "Why not?" delivered with a sigh, which he also took as good news. The fates were with him. The elevator—old, slow and less popular than the escalator—was empty.

"You're all set to bring some guy to his knees," he said by way of getting the conversation started.

"Oh, Will, I'm not so sure."

"Why?" He moved a step closer.

She moved a step away. "The probability of finding someone I'm hot for who's hot for me..."

"Earlier you sounded like you'd be hot for any man who was in your bed." As he said it, a flicker of doubt lit up a few of his brain cells. Was she really like that?

At the moment, he should be hoping she was, right? Because that gave him a chance with her, and he was getting hotter every second he spent with her. So why had he suddenly hoped she wasn't up for letting any Tom, Dick or Harry into her bed?

Forget it. There was only so much you could figure out in an elevator. He regained his proximity to Cecily and rested a hand against the wood-paneled wall, which put his arm right behind her shoulders.

When she stepped back, trying to get away, she got herself hugged instead.

She looked truly agitated. "I'm beginning to think it does matter. Let's not talk about it, Will, really."

"Okay," he said agreeably. "What would you like to talk about?" He didn't have to figure out what to say or how to say it. Cecily was setting herself up for a big surprise. What could be better?

HE DIDN'T MOVE HIS ARM. In fact, he leaned in a little closer. Cecily frantically groped for a neutral topic. "Let's talk about Muffy."

"Oh. Okay. What do you want to know about her?"

The elevator stopped on each floor. Shoppers got on, shoppers got off. "Well…" Cecily hesitated. "How long have you known each other?"

"All our lives," Will said, and his face was so close to her hair, she could feel his breath ruffle through it.

"All your lives. So your differences, your tensions, didn't come as any surprise to you?"

"Oh, no. We never got along. That's why my folks sent me to Exeter."

"To get you away from Muffy?" All this sounded very strange. Maybe Will was dumber than he looked—had to be to marry a woman he'd never gotten along with. Maybe she had a lot of money. Maybe she was really great in bed. *Don't go there.*

"Yep."

"But you got together again?"

"No way to avoid it."

"Yes, there is," Cecily cried. "You have to be strong! It's kinder to tell a woman the truth than to marry her and make her miserable with constant fighting."

"I know that," Will said.

She felt his smile against her hair. His mouth was much too close to her cheek. How many trips had they made up and down in this elevator? She felt as if she'd been stuck in there with him for most of her adult life.

"But it's too late now," she said miserably. "She's just had the baby, and as I've told you over and over, you need to be at the hospital with her, giving her your full support."

"But I'd rather be the man who gets to see you in that black thong."

Thank God the elevator was temporarily empty when he uttered those dire words. The thing she'd most dreaded had happened. She'd caught a man at a vulnerable moment and, because of her own selfish need to question him about attracting *other* men, had made him think she might be willing to satisfy his starved libido.

She felt sick inside. She'd made things worse by implying that she wasn't looking for anything lasting. He might be a bit on edge right now, but he was a good man inside. She could just feel it. And what he was thinking was that a temporary-fling type of woman wouldn't disturb the already uneven equilibrium of his marriage.

She felt like a piece of trash, but now she had to rise to the level of at least something worth recycling. "Will!" She flung his arm away and faced him, her eyes both hot and tearing up at the same time. "I was afraid something like this would happen. I'm horrified at myself, I'm ashamed and so, so, so sorry. I'm ashamed of you, too, but it's all my fault. And to answer your question, I absolutely will not go to bed—"

She stopped abruptly when the elevator doors

opened on five and two very pregnant women got on. The women gave them curious looks. Cecily wondered just how far her voice had carried.

"—until after the eleven o'clock news. So you can call me up to eleven-thirty—"

She paused again and spoke directly to the women. "I forgot. I'm in Dallas, in central standard time. That would be the ten o'clock news, so he can call me until ten-thirty." Even in her overemotional state, she could see the pregnant women were starting to look frightened. The world was whirling around her, and now the elevator was going down.

"Cecily…" Will said.

The women turned away. Cecily was sure they felt as comforted by the calm, deep voice as she was, sensing that even if they had a crazy lady on their elevator, they also had a man who could handle her.

She'd show them *she* could handle *him.* She tugged Will to the back of the elevator. "I mean it," she implored him, barely moving her lips. "Back off, now, while you're still clean. You can trust me. You never said it. It never happened."

"I don't want to back off," he whispered into her ear, setting off a fire alarm in her nervous system. "I don't need to back off. I'm not—"

They'd reached the first floor again. Cecily tried to leap out of the elevator, but Will had a firm hold on her. The pregnant women got off, whispering agitatedly to each other. Two elegantly dressed women stepped in and pushed the button for the third floor. Cecily looked them up and down and decided they were too self-absorbed to notice a warring couple at the back of an elevator. "You're not the man I thought you'd grow up to be," she fired at him. "I thought I could trust you, or I would never have laid out my personal problems in front of you."

"You should never trust a person you know as little about as you know about me."

"How right you are," she mourned.

They'd reached the third floor. The doors opened, but the two women didn't get off. Instead they whispered something to each other and pushed one of the elevator buttons.

Will lowered his voice. "So, let's get acquainted."

"On the elevator?"

"It won't take long."

"Will, this is very silly. I want to go to my room and—"

"Just follow my lead. Cecily, do you have brothers and sisters?"

"No."

"Pets?"

"Yes."

"Names?"

"Skip the names. Too many of them."

"Your turn now."

"Will, do you have brothers and sisters?" Cecily intoned.

"Yes."

"What kind? Brothers or sisters?"

"A sister. A *twin* sister."

"Name?"

"Margaret."

A little bell dinged in Cecily's head. "Margaret. Do you call her Margaret? Maggie? Or Marge?"

"Muffy," Will said and put his hands on either side of her head, turning her to face him.

Dumbstruck, she stared at him. "What are you saying to me?"

"Read my lips. Muffy…is…my…twin…sister."

The elevator doors opened and two more women got on. Cecily saw one of them eye Will and her speculatively before she faced front.

"Well, that's just sick," Cecily snapped.

"It's not sick. I'm not the father of my sister's baby. You thought I was, so I let you think it, and when you said you'd lied about what kind of doctor you were, I decided you deserved to think it. I pulled Muffy in on the job, but we knew we couldn't trust Mom and Dad to keep their mouths shut, so we got rid of them." With every word he drew her closer and her heart beat faster.

A couple of the shoppers turned around, looking startled. The others began to shift nervously. One quickly pushed a button. The elevator stopped on the next floor, and as a single unit, all of them got out.

In a shocked flash of memory, Cecily remembered the couple who'd exited the elevator at the hospital as she was getting on, the man's resemblance to Will and, she now realized, the woman's resemblance to Muffy. "Are you saying…?"

"I'm saying—" his arms went around her, both of them leaning against the back of the blessedly empty elevator "—that I'm free as a bird and ready for whatever you have in mind for the next twenty-four hours. If you'll have me."

She could hardly breathe. "You're not married to Muffy, and the child I so unwisely agreed to godmother is not your baby." Her heart pounded furiously as the elevator reached the top floor, halted and began its descent again.

"We can negotiate the godmother thing if you really don't want it, but not until the weekend's over." His gaze mesmerized her, and she closed her eyes. His hands caressed her shoulders, drew her closer, as his mouth hovered over hers then brushed her cheek, her forehead. At last his arms were around her, pulling her tightly to him, and Cecily melted in his embrace, flowing like liquid with the power of his desire. "We have to forget little Cecily and move on to big Cecily, wonderful Cecily, Cecily who needs exactly what I'd love to give her."

The elevator doors opened on the first floor and the security officer loomed in the doorway. This time he had backup, two more officers as burly as he, and behind them, the women who'd been their elevator companions formed a solid wall. "Hands above your head, sir, and get off the elevator."

"What's this all about?" Will said, letting go of Cecily and putting his hands in the air.

"We've received a complaint that you are molesting this woman."

"He may be a murderer!" said one of the women.

"He might even be the father of his sister's baby!"

The officer shook his head sadly. "What is the world coming to? I have to ask you, sir, to come along quietly."

"You owe me," Cecily said when she'd convinced the officer once again that Will was merely mentally disturbed—in a benign way, of course.

"I can't wait for you to call in your chits," Will said as they jaywalked across the street to the hotel.

She only hoped her legs would hold her up a few minutes longer. A miracle had happened. Will was hers for the weekend.

# 6

"CECILY CONNAUGHT," CECILY said to the man beneath the Courtland's brass Registration sign, then sent a sidelong glance toward Will, who'd gone to the other end of the gleaming black marble counter to check in.

"Will Murchison," Will said to the woman behind the counter, then sent a sidelong glance toward Cecily.

"The Shipley-Hargrove wedding party," Cecily said in unison with Will, then whipped her head back to stare at the nattily uniformed man behind the counter.

The registration man and woman sent sidelong glances toward each other.

"Your luggage arrived," the man said to Cecily, eyeing the many Sutherland's bags dangling from her hands, "and we've sent it up to your room. With your...shoes."

"Oh, thank heavens, somebody sent my sandals along," Cecily said. "I was afraid they were lost to me forever. You can burn the suitcase, for all I care."

"Good plan," Will said from his end of the counter.

"And we'll send your luggage up in a minute," the woman said to Will, giving him a sharp glance. "Warm day, isn't it?" she added, apparently reacting to Will's flushed face and tousled hair.

"Humid outside, isn't it?" Cecily's man said to her. She'd been gazing at Will. Now, looking down at

herself, she realized he was referring to her dress—
wrinkled, damp and sticking to her. Not that anything showed beneath her cotton bra. Which was a
good thing. Her condition resulted from the heat and
humidity of Will, not Dallas, and her body still
zinged from his touch. "Uh-huh," she said, hearing
Will say something quite similar.

"You've received a call," Cecily's man said to her
as Will's woman said the same thing to him. They
looked at each other.

"You both have voice-mail messages waiting," the
woman said, taking over.

"Thank you," Will answered in unison with Cecily.

The clerks handed over keycards in little folders
and wished them a pleasant stay at the Courtland.
Cecily felt their eyes boring into her and Will's backs
as they stepped briskly toward the bank of elevators.

"What's your room number?"

Cecily looked at the card. "Seven-oh-nine."

"I'm seven-seventeen."

"I'm sure Sally booked a block of rooms together,"
Cecily said.

But Will had halted in his tracks. "Not close
enough," he muttered and started back to the desk.

"But Will, they'll know…"

He wrapped his arm around her waist, pulled her
close and lightly touched his lips to hers. "Why
should a slut-puppy like you care?" He smiled.

It was a slow, lingering, teasing smile. What did it
mean? Had he figured out that this was her debut at
being a slut-puppy?

He gave her a quick kiss. "Go to your room and
start taking off price tags." He kissed her again.
"Then put on your favorite new thing."

HER ROOM WAS DECORATED IN English-country style, pretty and feminine, with a king-sized four-poster bed covered in a floral print trimmed in eyelet. She peeked out the window. The hotel, which from its exterior appeared to be a solid block, actually consisted of three wings around a kidney-shaped black pool. Now, in midafternoon, bronzed bodies filled the white chaises that surrounded the pool.

She backed away from the window and caught a glimpse of her familiar self in the full-length mirrors that covered the closet doors. Slowly she tugged her dress off over her head, then undid her clumsy bra and peeled it away from her damp skin. The cool air of the room washed over her like a caress, and she breathed a deep sigh of relief. She slid her panties down into a puddle at her feet, then picked them up. Holding the underwear that represented the utterly practical nature of her current life, she thought it would give her a clean-break sort of feeling to toss them out the window, then imagined them landing on the head of one of those bronzed bodies.

Would he look at the underwear with distaste, and say, "What are these? Orthopedic undies?"

Alas, the windows probably didn't open.

She let down her hair, brushed it out, then went to the bathroom to sponge her body with cool water. The soap was lemon-scented and refreshing as she dragged the cloth across her skin. She thought about how it would feel for Will to be holding the cloth, sliding it down her throat, her arms, her breasts, between her legs. It was an arousing image, one that made her long for Will's return.

Naked, she stretched out luxuriously on the bed, dragged one of her shopping bags close beside her

and began taking the new underthings out of their
tissue-paper wrappings. They felt wispy and feath-
erlight in her hands, filling her with a tingly sense of
anticipation.

Several minutes later, she faced the mirror wearing the pale blue lace ensemble Will had picked out
for her, had said she'd look good in, the bra and
panties no more than a web of soft, silky, slightly
stretchy lace exactly the color of a robin's egg. The
woman staring back at her was an unfamiliar person,
a new person. She raised her arms over her head,
spread her feet apart, let her hips sway from side to
side. She felt free. She felt…sexy.

A new, free, sexy woman who would soon be in
the arms of the man she'd never stopped wanting, a
man who had awakened her desires from their long,
long sleep. Still stretched out, she tightened her
hands into fists and held them aloft in a victory sign.
"I am tigress," she growled. "Hear me roar."

Her suitcase still lay open, and she pounced on it
tigerlike. "Die," she shouted at her white underwear
as she tossed dingy bras and panties into the waste-
basket near the desk. She dug a little farther and
pulled out a somewhat ragged sleep shirt. "You, too."
She gave it a toss.

Her suitcase was a mess. She'd packed in ten minutes, as usual, and everything she took out of it from
now on would be a surprise. A bad surprise. But that
untidy tangle of clothes belonged to her past—her
extremely recent past, admittedly, but nonetheless
over. Her future lay on the bed, all silk and lace. Pure
femininity.

Feeling better already, she made a snarly face at
the mirror and then gazed at herself again, suddenly

not quite satisfied with what she saw. Tigresses had more color than she did. She did own makeup—not that she ever wore anything but Bert's Bees lip balm. Knowing this, her mother had apparently spent hours and a fortune at a cosmetics counter in Saks— carrying pictures of Cecily, for heaven's sake—and had mailed Cecily a whole new face, complete with instructions on how to apply each of the numerous potions and powders and which of the numerous brushes to use for each. There was a typical note in the box that said, "Please, darling, for me, use this during the wedding festivities. You could be so pretty if you'd just try."

So Cecily made up her face, maybe for the first time since undergraduate school. Stroking on the pale pink lip gloss, she had to admit she looked more like a woman a man might want to make love with. Shivering with growing impatience, she carefully put away the rest of her new treasures and stretched out on the bed to wriggle against the soft cotton of the coverlet.

She was wriggling, increasingly hot and frustrated as she let her imagination take her into the near future, when two things distracted her. She had a voice mail waiting, and where the hell was Will?

WILL WAS STEPPING PURPOSEFULLY across the lobby, clutching the plastic key to his hard-won room— seven-eleven, which connected with Cecily's—when he recognized the man already waiting for the elevator. Sneaking up behind him, Will nudged the large Sutherland's shopping bag he held. "Congressman," he said. "Gotcha."

A low, desperate sound came from Congressman

Galloway's throat as he whirled to face Will. His face was as white as an arctic hare's. God, the man was goosey. Both Will's and Sally's parents were among his big supporters, financial and otherwise, and frequently entertained him in their homes. Even Muffy liked him. Will had never seen him get this nervous, even in an election year.

"Will," Galloway said weakly. "You're a man I haven't seen in a while." Slowly his face got a little color back.

Donald Galloway was twenty-five or so years Will's senior, but he'd laughed and joked with Will when he was a kid, and Will thought a little teasing wouldn't be out of order. "Yeah, but I saw you thirty minutes ago." Will gave him a sly smile. "Find something pretty for Nora in the lingerie department?" Hell, the man's face was going pale again. Will felt he'd misjudged and was presuming a camaraderie between them that didn't exist.

He suddenly felt like a naive fool. Maybe the lingerie hadn't been for Nora.

If Galloway was fooling around, Will didn't like the idea much, because Nora was a nice lady and her husband's biggest fan, but he sure wasn't going to tell. If he did, Nora would be the person he'd hurt the most. He thought he knew how to make the congressman feel more relaxed. "Tell you the truth," he said conspiratorially, "I would have spoken to you, but I was with a lady who preferred not to be seen shopping for underwear with me. Know what I mean?"

"Uh, sure, Will, sure."

He didn't seem to feel a whole lot better. His eyes had gone glassy. Will decided to be even more direct. "So I won't tell if you don't."

"Yeah, yeah," Galloway muttered. "Hey, I forgot. I need to buy shaving cream in the gift shop. See you later, Will."

He slunk away, a big change from his usual confident stride. Will was puzzled, but only one thing was on his mind right now. Not even Gus's finances could distract him, and certainly not the possibility that Congressman Don Galloway had a girlfriend on the side.

PACING THE ROOM IN HER BRA and panties, Cecily began to feel plagued by the blinking message light on the desk telephone. She knew the voice-mail message was from her mother. Her mother hadn't been completely convinced Cecily wouldn't find a plausible reason to skip out on the wedding.

Admittedly, her worry was justified. Cecily had indeed sinned in her heart when she'd told herself that if Vermont were to have an outbreak of mad cow disease, this would be an excellent time for it. Her father, at least, would understand that his daughter couldn't be in a wedding when her duty was to protect the meat-producing industry from financial ruin and thereby protect the very core of democracy—the GNP.

But no crisis had arisen and here she was. At the moment, she was extremely pleased she had come. *Elated* wouldn't be too strong a word. But the last thing in the world she wanted to do was talk to her mother. So she couldn't pick up the phone. If she picked up the phone and heard the message, she wouldn't be able to say, "Oh, sorry, I didn't get your call."

Which is what she planned to say. As she congratulated herself again on her irrefutable logic, she heard a knock on the door. And in her frantic dash to slip her dress back over her head, she realized the knock wasn't coming from the door to the hall but from the locked door that led to the next room.

"Cecily, unlock your door."

She let the dress fall to the floor. He had scored the connecting room. A thrill of heat passed through her. She stepped over to her door. "Say 'Rapunzel, let down your hair.'"

"I'm going to say 'Open, sesame' and kick the door in if you don't open it."

She smiled at the laughter in his voice and unlocked the door on her side. His boyish, gleeful smile faded. He stepped through the open door and slowly, like a man in a dream, rested his hands lightly at her waist, caressing the bare skin, devouring her with his gold-flecked gaze. "Lady," he said in a voice made thick from desire, as thick as sorghum molasses, "you have knocked me flat on my ass."

She was totally bowled over herself, and the man still had his clothes on. She put her hands on his shoulders and stroked the underside of his chin with her thumbs, watching his eyes darken. "None too romantic, but we're not really talking about romance here, are—"

His mouth swallowed the end of her sentence. His kiss was hard and deep, filled with need as consuming as hers. She kissed him back, claiming him as her prey, devouring the sweetness of his lips, the warmth of his skin.

His hands slipped up under her hair to caress her neck, trailed down her bare back to her waist, where he pressed her tightly against him. She felt the power and promise of his erection, and the ache inside her built explosively. Abruptly he broke off the kiss and relaxed his hold on her, his hands moving to the front closure of her bra. With excruciating slowness, he opened it, and her breasts fell free into his hands. Holding them, caressing them, his thumbs circling her peaked, throbbing nipples, he lowered his mouth to take hers. She opened to him, meeting the thrusts of his tongue, dizzy with desire.

"You're so beautiful." He backed her to the bed, where she collapsed with her arms stretched out to him. He yanked off his shirt and then covered her with his body, stroking her thighs, moving his hand between them.

Her breasts moved against crisp, chestnut hair and her hips instinctively thrust upward to meet his caress. The years fell away as if they'd never happened, and in her mind she was back in the groundskeeper's cottage, realizing a dream come true as their adolescent passions crashed around them more thunderously than the storm that raged outside.

He was everything she'd imagined he would be, a beautiful man, a warm man, her man—for now. She spread her legs, wanting more, hearing his gasp of pleasure as he slid his fingers inside her panties to touch her, found her wetness, knew the depth of her need.

He took his time, exploring, caressing, dipping down to kiss her mouth, her throat, her breasts, to run his tongue over the taut nipples, slipping off her panties to bury his face between her thighs. In a sudden agonized need for immediate release, she knew she wanted more of him. She wanted that hardness she'd felt, wanted him inside her. She was on the edge, falling, falling, falling....

"Does it feel good?" His voice was a murmur, gritty with arousal.

"Oh, yes." It was hard to get out the words.

"Am I doing what you like?"

"You're doing things...I didn't know how much I liked."

His laugh was low and soft. "Are we going too fast?"

"I want you inside me." She said it on a sob. She wanted him now, wanted him there for a long time, wanted to feel his pleasure as well as her own. He raised himself on one elbow and reached for his zipper, and in a few swift movements lay beside her, splendidly male, infinitely desirable.

Holding her breath, she touched him, heard him groan. He laved her with kisses—her face, her ears, her throat—while she stroked him lightly, tantalizingly, until she felt his impatience and knew she would soon possess all of him.

"You came prepared," she whispered as he protected himself and her.

He raised himself over her and stayed there for a moment, poised, gazing down at her with hunger in his eyes. "The Boy Scout type," he whispered back. "We are always prepared." And slowly, tormentingly, he entered her while, consumed by her own impatience, she lifted her hips to pull him in more deeply.

He filled her and surrounded her. She had thought she would possess him but instead was completely possessed by him. No one had ever made her feel this way, so totally embraced and cherished. He withdrew and thrust again and again, and with each thrust she felt more complete. It seemed they were beyond reality, locked in a world that was theirs alone.

The thrusts deepened, came faster, and she jousted with him in a battle both would win, until the aching pressure and heat built up feverishly and she was unable to hold back. With a cry she arched up to him and exploded in a tide of spasms that rocked her body, feeling the groan come from deep in his body as he, too, gave in to the pure pleasure of release.

Hot, panting and wet with sweat, they lay together in a tangle of sheets, separate, though, in their thoughts. At last he sighed deeply and stroked his hand between her breasts and down her belly. "You are some doctor, Cecily Connaught," he said, each word a warm stroke of its own.

She smiled at him. "Your condition requires many treatments, I'm afraid."

"That's good news. Because I was just thinking…"

He was fully erect again, throbbing against her thigh and tucking his arm beneath her to pull her over onto the length of his body when someone knocked none too discreetly on the door of his room.

"Don't answer it," Cecily said in a breathless whisper.

"It's the porter with my bag," he groaned.

"Clothes are the last thing you need right now." She got a determined grip on him.

"If I don't answer it, he'll come in. That's what porters do. They're supposed to walk right in and not notice us in the next room buck naked and rolling in the hay. It's your call, lady. I answer the door, or we give him the thrill of his life." His words puffed hotly against her skin.

The knock came again, even louder this time.

"Can you get the connecting door closed before he comes in?"

"No." He was already moving, rolling away from her, sliding out of bed, reaching for his pants, struggling into his shirt, and she could hear an ominous sound coming from the next room—the sound of a door opening.

She gave up. She couldn't quite face having sex in front of an audience. "Put a large bill in his hand and tell him you know how to work the air-conditioning and you're as happy to be here at the Courtland as he is happy to be your host."

He drowned out this sensible advice with a shout that might possibly have carried to a keen-eared Fort Worth resident. "Just a minute. Be right there." And he leaped toward the connecting door and closed it behind him.

FOR A MAN WHO'D BEEN YANKED straight from a dream come true—a dream of long, silky thighs, skin like heavy cream flavored with a drop of vanilla—to hideous reality, Will thought he was behaving pretty well.

It was particularly annoying to recall that all he had was one bag—a suit bag, and a *rolling* one at that. He hadn't needed a porter to bring it up. He could have managed with a duffle if he hadn't had to bring a dark suit for the party tonight and his monkey suit for the wedding.

The monkey suit was white. The whole wedding was white. "White on white," Sally had told him with a romantic sigh, which seemed to mean the whites didn't have to match, because his tux was very white and the satin lapels were—not very white and the pants were very white with a not-very-white stripe and the shirt was blindingly white—with ruffles that had some kind of stitch at the edges in the white of the lapels and stripes. He growled.

"Sir? Is anything wrong?"

"Oh. No." While these random thoughts had been running scattershot through his head, he'd been trying to remember where the hell he'd put his billfold, because in his haste to get to Cecily he recalled giving it a Frisbee kind of throw onto or into something or other. When he found it on the floor in one of his loafers, it took him another embarrassing minute to fumble out a ten-dollar bill—a ridiculous tip for one bag, but he'd read somewhere that guys did that when they were embarrassed. While he'd thought he was an exception to the rule, apparently he wasn't. At last the bill was in his fingertips, and he handed it to the porter.

"Thank you, sir. We're delighted to have you here at the Courtland. I hope you enjoy your stay."

Hadn't he heard that somewhere recently?

"May I show you the amenities of the room? This thermostat controls the—"

"Air-conditioning. I know. I'm sure I can figure out all the...amenities." He made an encouraging gesture toward the door. *Thank you. Now leave.*

"Perhaps you haven't noticed that you have a voice-mail message." Now the man looked more reproving than a man should look when he'd just gotten a ten-dollar tip.

"Yes, I know," Will muttered. *Leave, dammit, leave.*

"They told you at the desk, I think. You haven't checked it yet."

"But I will," Will said in a firmer, more forceful tone. "When I have time."

"I can show you how to access it if you—"

"All right!" He'd had it. "If I listen to the message, will you *leave?*"

"Of course, sir. I don't want to intrude on your privacy."

True to his word, he closed the door behind himself at last, but not until he'd watched Will pick up the phone. Will shook his head. Was there any business that didn't have some crazies in it?

Madder than hell, he pushed the message button.

"Will? Gator. Sorry I missed you at the hospital, but I wanted to ask you... Well, I know this sounds dumb, but when I was leaving Love Field, I thought I saw Gus getting on a private plane. Since I'm getting to the scene late and you know him a little better than the rest of us, I wondered if you knew what he might have been doing. Has anything gone wrong between him and Sally? Call me back in Muffy's hospital room." He repeated the number slowly. Twice. "Can't use my cell in here."

Shaken, Will put down the phone, consumed with guilt that he had managed to put Gus completely out of his mind and let Cecily completely fill it. He wanted the day to go on that way—filled with Cecily—and he gazed longingly at the door that separated him from her. Then with a muttered curse he returned Gator's call.

Gator answered with a cheerful, "I'll go outside and call you back on my cell. Stay put." Time passed while Will stayed put, shifting his weight from one foot to the other because he didn't want to be there, he wanted to be on the other side of the door where

Cecily was. But at last the phone rang and he snatched it up before it had done more than peep at him.

"You saw Gus getting on a plane?" Will asked, skipping the formalities, keeping his voice low and his back to the door.

"I thought it was Gus. I don't know the guy except for meeting him at a couple of parties. I guess nobody does except you, maybe. And it wasn't his plane, it was another one, a Learjet, so maybe I was wrong."

Will devoutly hoped so. The combination of possible tax fraud and Gus skipping town was making him crazy. "He was at the rehearsal. I don't think anything's wrong between him and Sally."

"That's good news."

Good news for Sally. Not necessarily good news for Will.

"You must know the guy better than I do," Gator said. "What's he like?"

"I don't know anything about him but his numbers." And those weren't adding up. "When we talk, he sounds like he's rapping with me, but when I look back, it turns out he hasn't told me a thing about himself. Whose plane was he getting on?"

"Well, I was in my car and thinking about Muffy and the baby, but the plane had a black-and-silver logo…let me think…something International. Shepherd. No, that's not it…."

"Think, Gator, *think*."

Gator thought. "It reminded me of wedding presents, that I'd forgotten to ask Muffy what we bought Sally and Gus. China, crystal, sterling. That's it— Sterling International."

Will sat down at the desk, reached for the phone pad and pen and scribbled down the name. Noth-

ing in Gus's tax information had included a company named Sterling International. What the hell
was it? And what was so important about it that it
had drawn Gus away from Sally on the eve of their
wedding?.

STILL NAKED, HOT, FRUSTRATED and impatient, Cecily
couldn't imagine what was keeping Will. Surely the
porter had left long ago. Had Will forgotten what
he'd been doing when he was interrupted?

She was finally impatient enough to go to the door
and open it just an inch, and what she saw made her
temper flare. With one touch he'd managed to turn
her on again, and now he was talking on the phone!

She marched straight to the desk and snatched up
the phone pad he'd been writing on. He jumped sky-
high. She stared at him, then wrote, "You still have
business with me."

She wrote it under the words Sterling International. He was working! What kind of one-night
stand was he, anyway?

He wrote on the pad: "Sorry, just a second." Into the
phone, he said, "Yeah, well, let me know if you find
out, um, anything, ummmm, about, uh, him or it."

"What's this?" she wrote and drew an arrow up
to the company name.

"Nothing important," he wrote. "Just another
minute, promise."

"E-mail me, okay? I'll get the computer set up.
Right," he told the receiver.

Cecily was grabbing for the pad, intending to
write exactly what she thought about his setting up
his computer and e-mailing at a time like this, but he
snatched it back. "Model your new nightgown for

me and wait for me in bed," he wrote. "I'll be right there." He added a slow, sexy smile and a caress that started at her shoulder and ran all the way down to her thigh. How could she say no?

She marched back into her room and, feeling more grumpy than sexy, put on the gown and robe. They were pale blue, like the lace lingerie, very sheer and very short. The gown was nothing more than a shapely little slip, and the robe was the same length, with satin trim down the front and at the hem of the kimono-style sleeves. It tied at the waist, but it didn't stay tied. It kept slipping open, silk sliding against silk…

She shivered. Silk sliding against skin, stroking her breasts, hardening her nipples, tickling her pubic hair, turning her on like a lover's caress.

Wow, Will really knew his undies.

She slid onto the bed and tried out several poses, then settled for sitting up against the pillows, one leg stretched out, the other drawn up in a way that wasn't blatant flashing but showed a bit of her bottom—quite accidentally, of course. This involved a good bit of thighs-rubbing-together action, which only intensified her impatience as she waited for Will.

Waited and waited and waited…

"Damn," she said and got off the bed. She opened her door and then Will's door. Will was off the phone—and on the computer!

"You are out here doing business instead of in there doing me?" she yelled at him.

He whirled away from the screen and leaped out of his chair. "Uh…I'm sorry. I mean I really do apologize. It's just this little situation that's come up…."

Fuming, she crossed her arms over her chest, then realized the effect was to shorten the gown and robe and dropped them back to her sides. "Seems to me your little situation has gone down rather than up."

He held out his arms imploringly. "Look, this is urgent. Not just important. Immediate. Believe me, this is not what I want to be doing right now."

She gazed at him. As much as she wanted to have a really big fight with him, what she wanted much, much more was to have sex with him right up until the rehearsal dinner.

She would simply have to seduce him.

# 7

WHEN HE SAID HE DIDN'T WANT to be doing this right now, that was God's own truth. She was almost edible in all that sheer blue stuff, and his hunger for her was nowhere close to being satisfied. Just his luck to find her again at the same time he was finding all kinds of reasons to worry about Gus's financial situation.

Not only was his professional reputation at stake, he also had a personal obligation to Sally. She was family. Their mothers were sisters. He couldn't sit by silently and let her marry a man whose financial situation was suspicious, nor could he let Gus break her heart by skipping the country with unreported, possibly illegal gains.

What he was doing was searching for information about Sterling International. Gus ran a security business. If Sterling International was a client, they might have summoned Gus because of an emergency, such as debugging the plane or checking out a bomb threat. Will just needed to know what the man was up to.

But even if he were engaged in something perfectly legal this afternoon, it still didn't explain the discrepancy between Gus's lifestyle and his reported income.

First things first, though. Will had found several

dozen companies with Sterling in their names and three called Sterling International. Gator might have misread or imagined the International part, so Will wouldn't restrict his search to those. He'd been going to one Web site after the other looking for clues and was anxious to get back to it.

But now Cecily was coming toward him, giving him a slow, meaningful smile, and her robe was coming open at the waist, giving him a full view through one layer of sheer blue silk of her small, perfect breasts with their tiny pink nipples hardened to points, her flat tummy centered by a neat little navel, the swell of her hips and, between her thighs, the mound of honey-blond hair that had tickled his mouth and tasted so sweet....

To his relief and gratitude, she slid her hands around his neck and gave him a light, off-center kiss. "I've been too selfish," she murmured into one corner of his mouth, which set everything stirring in his body that shouldn't be stirring when he was in the midst of a professional crisis. "If you have an emergency, of course it's more important than having fun with me."

"I like having fun with you," Will croaked, not letting himself touch her.

"Well, sometimes we just have to make sacrifices, don't we?" She moved up a little closer and the tight nipples brushed against him. "I know you want to take off your clothes and carry me back to that bed as much as I want you to." Her hips swayed forward, almost but not quite touching him. "But people have to take work seriously, don't you think?"

Oh, God, she was even closer, and with her arms around his neck, the gown and robe were riding up higher and higher. Will tried as hard as he could not to put his arms around her, but he failed. He settled his hands lightly on her back. The silk must be slippery, because his hands kept sliding down toward her delicious bottom when he'd intended to keep them high on her shoulder blades.

"Don't you worry. When you think you can take a little break from your work, I'll be ready and waiting for you." She punctuated the word *ready* by taking that last fatal step forward and wriggling ever so lightly against his aching erection. The last drop of blood left in his brain cells flew south like a Canada goose. "I'll snuggle up against you, and then I want to kiss you all over your body—and I mean all over."

His hands took the last fatal slide and his fingers closed over taut, silky-skinned, bare buttocks.

He actually gasped aloud.

And then he thought about Gus and he thought about Sally. He thought about Sally's failed first marriage and his aunt Elaine's grief when it had ended.

And then Cecily moved against him again, a little more suggestively.

*Gus,* he thought desperately. *Sally, my job, my family's peace of mind are all at stake here.*

"I..." he said, "I...have to do just a little bit more work." And he managed to let go of her delicious bottom, spin himself around and sit back down at the desk, throbbing uncomfortably, to bring up his e-mail.

He felt an electrical storm brewing behind him, but she surprised him. "I understand," she said, all kindness. "I have things to do, too. I haven't tried on even half of my new underwear. You go ahead and work." She slid her arms around his neck, tucked her hands inside his shirt and splayed them across his chest, almost but not quite touching his nipples, playing in his hair.

He gritted his teeth and entered his password.

"I especially want to try that pretty little apricot-colored set," she purred, dropping a kiss on his ear. "I'll be back in a few minutes."

She left. Will thought about locking his door, but that seemed childish. Gator hadn't sent an e-mail message, so he went back to the Internet, returning to a Web site for Sterling, Inc. This company was located in Montana, was owned by a man named Sterling and made things out of sheepskin.

Who'd want to steal a sheepskin?

"Where to look next?" he muttered.

"At me," Cecily said from a spot too close behind him.

It rattled him, but he turned around to see her in the camisole and panties that were the pinkish color of salmon, the camisole doing nothing to conceal her breasts and the panties so narrow that a few strands of crisp, curly, dark gold hair peeked out above them.

"How do I look in this?" she said, her eyes glittering.

"Very nice," he managed to say. Even his throat felt swollen. He was hit by a brilliant thought. "But I haven't seen you in that black thong yet. Try it on for me."

She slithered back into her room. He closed his eyes and moaned, then opened his e-mail again.

Still nothing from Gator. He e-mailed a friend who was a professor at the business school at New York University, and revealing as little as possible, asked him how to go about finding out if a company owned a plane and employed a security agency. Just as he clicked the Send button, he felt Cecily's hands cover his eyes.

"Surprise," she said into his ear, vibrating every nerve ending in his body.

Those were her naked breasts brushing his shoulders. He could tell without looking. He leaned back against them, then turned to sneak a peek at her.

"You didn't say which bra I should model."

"No," Will groaned. "No, I didn't."

"So I didn't wear one. What do you think?"

Reluctantly he turned around, and so did she, and his gaze was suddenly filled with the ultimate butt, round but with well-toned firmness, like the butt of a woman who worked out regularly.

Or delivered calves regularly.

Or a woman who was often in the arms of a man, lifting to meet his thrusts, her legs spread to draw him in deeply, twisting, turning, struggling in an agony of desire...

He was wasted. He gave up. His hands closed on those creamy cheeks, kneading them, lifting them— and from his laptop came a little ping.

His hands stilled, then dropped away from her, and he clenched the back of the chair. Like a man in a dream, he turned back to the laptop. The ping meant he had a new message, maybe from Gator.

His hand was on the mouse, bringing up Mail and Newsgroups, when in one fluid motion Cecily poured herself over him, straddling him, her hair loose and flowing, hiding the screen, her breasts crushed against his chest, making him suddenly uninterested in the screen, the e-mail, Gator or Gus.

She felt hot, aflame with a need too intense to play games anymore. She was desperate for the sex—even more desperate than he was. He could feel it in the way she sought out his swelling erection and moved against him, slow and languid but purposeful. He had to satisfy her, at least cool the flames inside her with one moment of relief.

And so he held her, moving with her, his face buried in her throat and his hands on her bottom, lifting her, stroking her, raking her with his fingernails. He felt her come in a series of violent shudders, with a moan from low in her throat, just as he glimpsed over her shoulder the e-mail address at the top of the screen.

While she clung to him, he snaked a hand out to the mouse and opened the e-mail from Gator. It was a short, simple, chilling statement.

Gus was missing.

IT WAS A PECULIAR POSITION to be in—Cecily sitting on an erection that was still the size of the Chrysler Building and him with a professional problem the size of a small civil war.

He couldn't talk to her about the problem. She'd learn soon enough that Gus was missing, but discretion forbade him to tell her what Gus's disappearance meant to him.

She stopped moving against him and gave him a little shake. "Will, still here?" Her mouth was swollen, her eyes heavy-lidded, her voice smoky. She was irresistible—nearly.

"Sure." He tried for a wide, sexy smile, but his eyes kept drifting toward his laptop screen.

"So maybe you'd like to continue this activity instead of *staring at your e-mail?*" Her eyes were starting to flash and her voice rose with every word. He was in big trouble.

He tucked her head against his shoulder and ran his fingertips down her back. He could see the screen better with her hair out of the way. "Oh, yeah. That was just a sample. In just a minute, right after I look at this one little thing, we'll do some more sampling, and then…"

*Gus was missing. Had Gator asked all the right questions? Had he tracked down the best man, that Derek guy, and asked him where he thought Gus might have gone?*

Derek Stafford's connection to Gus was a professional one. Will had inferred that they'd worked together in the past, which was why Gus had asked him to be best man, and maybe Derek still served as a consultant in Gus's new security business. Other than those assumptions, none of their mutual friends knew any more about Stafford than they knew about Gus.

His lap was suddenly, sadly, empty, and Cecily was standing behind him. He could tell she was madder than hell without even turning around to look at her. "Sure we will," she said. "I know your definition of 'a minute.'" She flounced away, opened his door, opened her door, slammed his, slammed hers, and Will was left with an empty lap, a classic case of blue balls and a whole lot of silence.

His door flew open. She was back. "I have never, *never* known a man so attached to his clothes and his computer as you." She huffed for a second. "In fact, you're so boring, I'm going to find out who my voice-mail message is from and call her back, *even though I know it's my mother!*"

Muffy's words came back to him as if she'd yelled them at him only yesterday: "You're about as much fun as phonics!"

But he didn't feel as though he could kill Cecily as

he had Muffy. He wanted to drag her off to bed and make love with her until she screamed.

CECILY GAVE WILL'S DOOR AN especially emphatic slam and then did the same thing with her own. The moment of relief had given way to suddenly building desire to be skin to skin with him, to have him inside her again, deep inside her, thrusting inside her while she writhed against him. He wasn't having the same vivid, arousing image. He wasn't interested in anything but his work.

It had always made her a little uneasy to think of her parents having sex, but now she realized she didn't need to feel uneasy, because her father probably did this same thing to her mother all the time.

And really, what right did she have to complain? Didn't she put work before everything else? The only reason she was free this weekend was that it was difficult to impossible to bring her patients with her.

If she could have, she would have brought Bertha the sow, who would soon give birth to the biggest litter she'd ever had, and Cecily had predicted complications. With Bertha's condition to monitor, she had to admit sex with Will would have been second on the list in order of importance.

She unclenched her fists, anger giving way to disappointment and frustration. Also, the thong was a torture device, undoubtedly invented by men. She took it off, then looked through her new lingerie again and put on the lace panties like the blue ones, but in white. From her suitcase she took a shirt she liked, a long-sleeved blue-and-white stripe—well, more blue and grayish by now—and put it on, relaxed by its much-washed softness.

Still reluctant to face the real world, she picked up the phone, pushed the message button and lay down on the rumpled bed, resigned to the sound of her mother's voice.

"Cecily, we don't really know each other yet, but—"

She sat bolt upright. True, her mother didn't really know her, but this was not her mother.

"—this is Gus, and I need your help."

Something was wrong. Her heart pounded. She slung her legs over the side of the bed and slid them into her Teva sandals, ready to run if she needed to, reminding herself she would need to put on pants first. But something in Gus's voice told her he wasn't sending her out to buy eye-makeup remover for Sally.

"I had to leave town for the afternoon. I didn't tell Sally, didn't have time for an argument, so she'll go ballistic when she finds out I wasn't at the golf course with the rest of the guys. I thought maybe since you were the maid of honor and her oldest friend, you'd be the right person to call her. Tell her I'm fine, this is just a little job I had to do, and I'll be back in time for the rehearsal dinner, okay? And tell her I love her more than ever. It's not like I'm leaving her at the altar. Thanks. See you tonight."

Cecily began to relax. It wasn't a crisis after all. Sally would be royally ticked off for sure—the very idea of a man working on the day before his wedding—

The similarity between Sally's situation and her own was striking, come to think of it. Gus had a higher priority than his imminent marriage, and Will had a higher priority than Cecily's sex life.

Men.

Just for the heck of it, Cecily went through her

suitcase, her medical bag and her purse looking for the schedule of events for the weekend, but couldn't find it. Seeing Will's name in the wedding party roster had rattled her badly. She must have left it on the plane. She'd immediately decided not to join the bridesmaids for the spa afternoon—a spa afternoon ranked right up there with a root canal—had memorized the times and places for the rehearsal, rehearsal dinner and wedding and had promptly forgotten the name of the spa.

But it wasn't that important. She was just letting Sally know Gus wasn't jilting her. So she'd leave a message for Sally in her room, the honeymoon suite, where Sally's mother was forcing Sally to stay alone tonight.

Mothers.

The hotel operator connected her to Sally's voice-mail, where she quoted Gus's message verbatim. Then she went back to her tangled suitcase to get the book she'd brought to read—*Syngamus Trachea, Recent Strides in Prevention*—by a famous veterinary professor.

The room was cool, the bed was comfortable and a study of parasites wasn't something destined to turn a person on, but she couldn't focus on worms— at least not those of the parasitic variety. Gus and Will both qualified as worms of the *Homo sapiens* sort. She had reasons to be mad at Will, but didn't know why she suddenly felt uneasy about Gus.

Of course, with her attitude toward marriage, she was just looking for something to go wrong. He might be buying something beautiful for Sally—diamonds or a new car. He hadn't sounded scared or worried. But had his lazy drawl sounded a bit rushed? That was understandable, wasn't it? He had to do what he had to do and get back for the rehearsal dinner.

She read another page. Then she decided she'd feel better if she spoke to Sally personally. Maybe Will had brought the itinerary. Accounting, lawyerly types did that kind of neat, organized thing. Clutching the book, she opened both connecting doors and stepped into Will's room. "Gus called," she said.

She certainly wasn't prepared for Will's reaction. He levitated straight up from the desk chair, whirled, rushed over to her and grabbed both her arms. "You should have told me. I need to talk to him."

She was too startled to answer for a second or two. "It was just a message on the voice mail," Cecily said. "The one I was so sure was from my mother. Why are you so—"

"What did he say? Where is he?"

"I don't know where he is," she said, trying to calm Will, "but he's fine. He wanted me to tell Sally not to worry about him, that he'd be back for the rehearsal dinner."

"Did he say why he left?"

"He said he had a little job to do. Really, Will, you're overreacting, especially for a man who seems to have a few little jobs of his own to do." She glared at him.

"Sorry," he said hurriedly, dropping his grip on her arms. "How did he sound?"

What an exasperating man. "He sounded like an airline pilot, you know, that fake good-old-boy voice they use when they're saying the plane's encountering some turbulence and would we please fasten our seat belts and pray."

"But did he sound like the pilots do when they're telling the truth or the way they sound when they're lying and the plane's about to crash?"

Cecily gritted her teeth. "I can't really answer that penetrating question, Will. I've never been on a plane that was about to crash."

"In the movies," he said, ignoring her sarcasm. "You know what I mean."

She tightened up her mouth, but she did think about it. "Marginally more like a pilot who's lying and trying to sound soothing."

Will snapped his fingers. "Just as I thought."

Cecily simply snapped. "Thought what? And by the way, I resent that even half-naked I can't drag you away from your job, while Gus has you forgetting all about your work simply by leaving town fully dressed."

He held out his arms in a gesture of appeal. "Cecily, Gus *is* my work."

HE WAS BREAKING EVERY RULE in the book by telling Cecily why he was more than worried about Gus. But even when she was glaring at him, she looked so sweet and friendly in her blue-and-white striped shirt that he couldn't help himself. Somewhere inside him he knew he could trust her, and he'd been worrying alone as long as he could handle it.

"Whew," Cecily said when he'd finished his short, blunt statement that he suspected Gus had income from some source other than his security company and that Muffy's husband, Gator, had seen him at the airport, apparently flying somewhere. "That puts a different spin on his leaving town the day before his wedding."

"Doesn't it, though." He didn't protest when Cecily dragged him down to the sofa, sat close beside him, crossed her long, slim, bare legs and reached for another pad and pencil that lay on the coffee table beside another telephone.

"Start at the beginning," she said. "What worried you about Gus's tax return?"

He observed with some surprise that in this mode, no longer brazenly seductive but simply supportive, Cecily was for some mysterious reason even more desirable. An enveloping warmth and a strength that made her seem Amazonian emanated from her. This was a woman who'd back him up if he had to trade a friendship for professional ethics. He let himself snuggle shoulder to shoulder with her, reminded himself that business had top priority over pleasure and then came out with everything.

"He sent me his tax information. He pays himself a salary from the security company proceeds, and it's right in line with the reported profits—decent but not exorbitant. He has the middle-class person's stock portfolio, also decent, but he's not quite a millionaire."

"Sounds fine so far."

"So what about the Lamborghini? And the classic Citroën? And the house in Highland Park? And the country club memberships. Skiing time-shares, travel, Rolex watches and Armani suits. The clues I've gotten from my mother and Muffy go on and on."

"He's spending a lot more than that decent income could pay for?"

"Looks like it. Then there's his plane…"

"But he deducts that from the security company grosses."

The woman was sharp, but he had the numbers.

"More than the company could afford with those grosses."

"Sally's loaded," Cecily said without the slightest indication of envy. "She has trust funds out the wazoo."

"Mr. Shipley insisted on a prenup. Gus thought it was great. Sally was embarrassed."

The way Cecily's perfect forehead creased when she was puzzled began to entrance him. They were alike in some ways. He was sure his forehead creased in the same way and his eyes squinted up in the same way when he was working out a problem. When a problem arose, she seemed to care about solving it as much as he did. And this was a really big problem.

"Did he leave in *his* plane?" she asked him, pencil poised.

"No." His conscience bleeped at him like a pager. Should he tell her absolutely everything or not? At this point, why the hell not? "The plane had a Sterling International logo. I've never heard of the company, so I've been looking at companies called Sterling on the Internet."

"That's a start," Cecily said. "But how will you know when you find the right one? There must be dozens."

"I have no idea," Will said, feeling pretty glum.

"My first responsibility is to Sally. I have to talk to her in person," Cecily said with an air that said "don't mess with my priorities." "In fact, that's why I came out here—to see if you knew where the bridesmaids were going this afternoon."

"You didn't get the schedule of events?" Why Sally hadn't included Cecily in the luxurious spa afternoon distracted him briefly from his big problems.

"Of course Sally sent me a schedule of events," Cecily said crossly. "It grossed me out. It was a chatty little letter from her and Gus telling the wedding party what their perks were. Like members of a wedding party deserve perks. And what fun everyone was going to have. How do they know what they think is fun will be fun for everybody else? Anyway, I had no intention of going to the spa, so I didn't bother remembering its name." She paused. "The name of a spa isn't the kind of thing that sticks in my mind. Ask me to remember the names of twenty-five known stomach parasites—that I can do."

"As enlightening as that sounds, we'll do it some other time," Will said. Now he was thoroughly distracted. Cecily, who'd sounded like a woman who'd been exiled from the bridesmaids' treats of facials, hair coloring, manicures and pedicures, was telling him she'd excluded herself on purpose because she didn't need all that stuff.

He also noticed that she'd glanced guiltily at her toes. He couldn't see anything wrong with her toes. The nails weren't polished, but the toes looked as long, slim and suckable as the rest of her.

Forget the toes, he said firmly to the lower half of his body. Gus was his top priority right now.

"I didn't read the itinerary," he confessed. "The first sentence put me off. Something like, 'Hey, Dudes and Divas, we're gonna have us a hell of a wedding weekend.'"

"I found it annoying, too," Cecily said primly.

"So I just wrote down the times for the rehearsal, the dinner and the wedding."

Cecily gave him a focused gaze that almost wiped out all his good intentions of making sure Sally would be marrying a decent man—and he, Will, would be signing an honest tax return. "I saw your name and stopped there," she said.

It rocked him to the core. It was the time to say something significant, something that would change the whole atmosphere of their time together. But he couldn't come up with it fast enough. Cecily was already on to the task at hand.

"I'll look up spas in the Yellow Pages," she said.

Will made a dive for the drawer that held phone books. He was infused with an urgency to get the problem to a reasonable stopping point—stopping for the thing he really wanted, which was Cecily naked in his bed or hers and the other parts of their lives moving smoothly along without them.

No, he wanted a little more. He wanted to establish her back in his life. The next twenty-four hours would do nothing more than whet his appetite.

With the phone books, he sat on the sofa, just a little too close to her. He was gratified when she moved a little closer to him, too, and thrilled when she slipped off her sandals and tugged her feet up under her thighs, the Yellow Pages resting on her lap and her head resting on his shoulder.

Cozy. He slid an arm around her.

"Spas," she said, but her voice was rich and dreamy, and again he experienced that sense of animal strength in her. Animal in that she focused intently on what she wanted at any given moment— and at this moment, she wanted to help him while feeling close to him. Watching her thumb through the pages for the S section and begin to browse through an endless list of spa entries heated him up even more than the black thong had.

It was as if they were a team. A couple. A couple

who had sex and a whole lot of other things keeping them together.

And he'd lost his head and was thinking way out of the box, which as everybody knew was not the kind of thing an accountant—especially an accountant whose client might be cheating on his tax return—should be doing.

Didn't mean he had to stop cuddling Cecily. Awareness of all aspects of the situation—that was the ticket. List the tasks, then prioritize them.

That was his current problem—prioritizing them.

"What are you looking for?" he asked her, tightening his hold on her such a little bit he hoped she wouldn't notice.

"Something that rings a bell." Her profile told him she was drawing her light brown, arched brows closer together as she studied the phone book.

He felt too warm again. She was working on *his* problem, was willing to help *him* solve it, and he wasn't helping *her* at all.

"I read the whole agenda," she said, "so the name of the spa would have made some sort of impression in my mind. I'm hoping I'll see it and think 'that's the one.'"

"Is there anything that might jog your memory?" He was thinking about Gator saying, "Wedding presents...sterling." Seeing the puzzled look on her face, he added, "Did the name remind you of something else? A book? A movie?"

She looked up at him so suddenly that their mouths hovered together like butterflies in flight. "America the Beautiful," she whispered in a smoky voice, her breath warm and sweet against his lips, then quickly looked down at the phone book.

Will took it off her thighs, cuddled her a little closer and found he needed to clear his throat before he spoke. "American Spa," he said, starting off at the top of the list.

"No."

"Beautiful You Day Spa."

"No."

"Spacious Skies Day Spa."

"There can't be a Spacious Skies Day Spa."

"No, there isn't," he said, checking the S listings. "There is a Big Sky Day Spa."

"That's not it."

He went back to the A listings. "What about Amber's Salon?"

"No. Why Amber?"

"Amber waves of grain."

"Of course. And purple mountains' majesty above the fruited—"

"Purple Plains Day Spa. No mountains."

"Maybe we should sing the song all the way through. I know the words. I can't carry a tune, though."

Singing hadn't been part of the weekend culture at Green Trails Stable. "That's what everybody says. I'm sure you have a great voice. Oh, beautiful..." Will began.

"For spacious skies..." Cecily chimed in.

She was right. She really couldn't carry a tune. How could someone with such a beautiful, sultry speaking voice sound so terrible when she was singing?

"For amber waves of..."

The first stanza failed to awaken the memory of the name of the spa, and Will's eardrums were aching. "Maybe we should bite the bullet and go down the list one name at a time," he suggested.

"Did you see how many spas are on that list? I remember the words to the next stanza. I'll sing it. Oh, beautiful, for patriots' dreams that see beyond…"

Listening to Cecily's rendition of the second stanza was a painful experience. Why did it make him hug her a little tighter?

"…the years. Thine…Alabaster Day Spa!" she shrieked so suddenly they both almost fell off the sofa. Righting herself she grabbed the phone book out of his hands and frantically punched in the number.

"I understand your promise to your guests is to protect them from their everyday interruptions," Cecily said a few minutes later, after she'd asked for Sally and stressed the importance of reaching her. "But this isn't an everyday interruption. In fact, it's something of an emergency, so I'd appreciate it very much if you'd get her off the warm-oil-massage table and put her on the phone."

Will was worried about how pink her face was getting and even more concerned when her knuckles on the phone began to turn white.

"I can see your point there, too," she said with a sweetness that wasn't backed up by anything in her body language, "that if Sally were expecting an emergency call from me she'd have given me her cell number…."

Apparently she was repeating the conversation for his benefit, because she turned to him, rolling her eyes.

"But you see—" her voice started to rise "—how the hell was she supposed to guess she'd have an emergency, know what I mean? That's what an emergency is, isn't it? Something that happens suddenly and without warning? That needs to be handled quickly? So get the woman on the phone. Now!"

Will knew that would have done it for him, and apparently it did it for the Alabaster Day Spa receptionist. While she waited, Cecily muttered imprecations to herself, but her skin tone was returning to normal and she'd switched the phone to her other hand and was flexing her fingers.

She abruptly stopped flexing. "She what? She did. How long ago? Can you catch the limo?" She drooped all over. "Okay, well..." She gritted her teeth. "Thanks so much for trying."

She slammed the phone down. "While that...that airhead argued with me, Sally and her bridesmaids walked right past her and out to the limo."

"Undisturbed by everyday interruptions," Will said. He went horizontal on the sofa, arms and legs stretched out.

Cecily stayed at the desk, her forehead resting on one hand.

Her hands, when she'd touched him, had the same controlled strength he saw in the rest of her. Those hands had delivered baby lambs and piglets, lifted sick and wounded animals. She was different from anyone he knew. She was a special person. Special and especially sexy. And he'd recognized it even when he was an adolescent, testosterone-driven, mindless organism.

He opened his eyes and looked at her at the same moment she lifted her head and looked at him. "I was just thinking," he said, slowly getting into a more upright position.

"So was I," Cecily said, uncrossing her legs, clearly planning to stand up.

"That we've done all we can for now," Will said, getting up to meet her.

"Right, we've done all we can. We have to wait for Sally to get the message in her room," Cecily said.

"And Gus will be back for the rehearsal dinner, so I can ask him right up front instead of nosing around behind his back, just a simple, 'Hey, Gus, what's Sterling International?'"

Cecily glanced at her watch. "You'll have to wait a while to do that. Are you sure you can handle it?"

Will put his hands on her shoulders and brushed his lips across hers. "I have never," he said, pulling her a little closer and sliding his arms around her, "been so sure," he continued, giving her a more purposeful kiss, "of anything in my life."

AT LAST SHE LAY BESIDE HIM again, the warmth of his skin and the prickle of the crisp hair on his chest and legs exciting her to near madness. She was getting exactly what she'd wanted but not what she'd expected. She'd expected to prance around in sexy underwear and be excited, then satisfied, by erotic words, technical competence and her own deprived libido. Instead she was being stroked by a real man, excited by his desire and her own—a man who seemed to like her body, maybe even liked her.

The way he caressed her breasts—circling her nipples with his tongue, moaning softly as if every second of the delight he was giving her pleased him just as much—stirred both her body and her heart. He made her feel not merely desired as any man might desire a woman but cherished.

That feeling of being cherished collapsed every defense against personal involvement she had at her disposal, and she gave herself completely to the sensations and emotions that were taking over. Heat and moisture flooded to the apex of her thighs, and she trusted him enough to let those reactions carry her away, let her mind go free in his arms.

His hands, his mouth on the most secret, private parts of her, inflamed her, and when at last, having driven her over the peak again and again, he entered her to give himself release at last, the flames burst even higher, and she came with him in a glorious burst of fireworks.

The entire concept of a one-night stand fled in the explosion, and Cecily accepted the terrible truth that she needed Will for much more than twenty-four hours. She might even be in love.

# 8

"LET'S NOT GO."

"Okay," Will said.

"You can call Gus. You don't have to see him."

"Right."

"Just say, 'Gus, what are you up to?' Not like a fickle, faithless friend who's trying to mess up the wedding but like an outraged cousin who'd rather mess up a wedding than let Gus mess up Sally's life."

"Um."

"Or we could tell Sally's father we're worried. He wouldn't have to pretend to be an outraged father. He does outrage naturally, my mother tells me."

"Uh-huh."

"Besides, so many people will be at that rehearsal dinner, they won't even miss us," Cecily said.

"Never miss us," Will said.

Cecily rose up on one elbow to gaze at him. He was supine, lying on his back with his eyes closed. She ran her fingertips down his chest, tangling them in the crisp, curly chestnut hair, then drew little circles around his navel.

He moaned.

She paused, fingertips poised over the flat plane of his stomach. "You okay?"

"Where are you getting all this energy?"

She resumed her stroking. "Oh, this takes hardly any energy at all. Now this—" she slid over him "—this takes effort."

He yawned. Not encouraging.

"Food," she said. "That's what you need. We can order from room service." Her mouth suddenly watered for real Texas nachos loaded with beef and cheese, sour cream, guacamole and salsa. "I could handle a nacho or two." She sat up, still straddling him, and reached for the hotel directory of services in hopes of finding a room-service menu. Thumbing through the pages, she glanced down at him. "Ah. I see the nachos got your attention."

His eyes still closed, he smiled. It was the most action she'd gotten out of him in the last fifteen minutes.

"Oh, look, a menu at last. Okay, how about nachos and an order of fajitas with all the trimmings?"

"Two orders. Each."

"Three words," she said. "I can tell you're in a state of hysterical excitement. What do you want to drink?"

"Beer. Goes well with Tex-Mex."

"Beer it is."

She reached for the phone just as it rang. "You don't suppose room service is calling *us*, do you?" And then she said, "Mother! Hi!" She scrambled off Will, who said, "Oof," almost loudly enough for her mother to hear, retreated to the other side of the bed with the telephone and pulled the sheet up to her chin. Will turned on his side to face her. He looked amused. She switched to the speaker phone. Let Will see for himself how amusing it was to talk to her mother.

"At last. I can rest easy tonight. My daughter is

alive and speaking to me. You might have called when you got there."

"I've been busy."

"For all I knew," her mother said, "you might have backed out at the last minute. Your father wouldn't let me call any earlier. He said, 'Samantha, of course she'll go, so don't bug her.' But I said, 'Fred, I'm her mother. I have to hear her voice to be sure—'"

"You've heard it, so you know I came."

"About fifty times," Will said.

Cecily rolled over and clapped her free hand across his mouth. "See, you worried for no reason at all."

"Is there a man in your room, Cecily?"

"Just Dan Rather."

"Oh." Instead of relieved, her mother sounded disappointed. "He's already married, isn't he?" Now a wistful note entered in. "Is Sally glowing with happiness?"

Cecily frowned at the phone. Instead of parenting methods, her mother had mastered method acting. "Utterly radiant," she said. "The perfect bride." *Absent a groom for the moment.*

"Just as you will be one day," her mother said. "I hope."

"Never, Mother. You can delete your folder of wedding ideas."

Will gave her an odd look.

"Did you have a productive afternoon at the spa?"

Cecily winced and crossed her fingers. "I had a great afternoon." At least it made Will smile again.

"I hope so." Now the motherly mood was one of worry. "I hope you had your hair done and a manicure and a pedicure. I know you can't get those things done properly in Vermont."

"No," Cecily said patiently, "up there I just cut my hair with a scythe and my nails with pruning shears."

"That's what I thought the last time I saw you." She let out the resigned sigh of a martyr. "Well, darling, now that we've talked I feel much better. Have a lovely evening, and I hope we can spend a minute with you before the wedding tomorrow. We're taking the earliest plane. I'm so sorry we couldn't come today, but there was the matter of the paper Daddy had to give."

"Yes. Daddy's paper." Cecily said goodbye, and pushed the speaker phone off.

Will was gazing at her, looking curious and thoughtful. "You told your mother you were never going to get married."

"As I have told her repeatedly."

"What makes you so sure?"

Cecily tugged the sheet up a little farther. "Living with them. With my parents. Watching them."

"They don't get along?"

"They don't fight like you and Muffy do. Or did. They just move along parallel lines. They don't connect."

"But they stay together. They must have something going."

"I don't know what it is. Except plenty of money. There's family money on both sides, but Daddy pursues his academic career as if it were the only thing standing between him and welfare. He makes money, Mother spends it and he doesn't pay the slightest attention to her, ever. He communicates with his colleagues and his students but mostly with his own brain, and she communicates with her women friends, her hairdresser and her decorator. They never communicate with each other. As I said, parallel lives."

"I guess lots of marriages drift like that," Will said.

"When one person has sacrificed a career for the marriage, yes, I think they do. Okay, enough sociology, let's order food before anything else happens."

Right on cue, the phone rang again. With a disgusted snort, Will got out of bed. "You take your call, I'll order from my room."

Cecily took a second to admire his magnificent naked backside before she picked up the phone. She wished she'd taken another second to sigh and drool, because the voice on the phone came at her like an electrical shock.

"Thanks for the call, but he's not back and the rehearsal dinner starts in fifteen minutes! What the hell am I supposed to do? Go to my own rehearsal dinner without a date?" And with that, Sally burst into tears.

WILL WALKED BACK INTO CECILY'S room no longer exhausted. He'd added a few more things to their room-service order, and the evening seemed filled with promise. He stopped short at the door, though, because he could see that Cecily was in the midst of a disaster. As if it would help, he got a towel from the bathroom and wrapped it around his waist, a prehistoric warrior girding himself for battle and protecting his only truly essential body part.

"Sally," Cecily was saying soothingly, "all I know is what Gus told me. He said he loved you more than ever. Things happen, you know? Maybe he's in a traffic jam in a no-service area, so he can't call you on his cell. This is the eve of your wedding. You have to have faith in him."

"Bull," Will said, and Cecily shushed him with a finger on her lips.

"He definitely said it was a job he had to do," she said after a long silence at her end of the line. Then her voice faltered a little. "Yes, he did say out of town—"

Another long silence. "The security business isn't a nine-to-five job, Sally, and something came up—" The phone nearly leaped out of her hand from the decibel level of Sally's response.

"Of course I will. Absolutely." She was speaking into the receiver, but she finished the sentence looking straight at Will. "Wouldn't miss it for the world, especially not now when you need all the support you can get. We'll…I'll be a little late. My hair's not cooperating. Now calm down, Sally. Remember what a gracious and charming person you are, and you'll get through this dinner like the lady your mother taught you to be." She stuck her finger in her mouth and pretended to be gagging.

Will threw both arms in the air—so much for the nachos and fajitas, because she was obviously talking about the rehearsal dinner—and the towel fell off, revealing how ready he was to make love with Cecily some more, much more and as quickly as possible. He grabbed the towel off the floor, went briefly into his own room and returned with a shaving kit. Marching into Cecily's bathroom with as much dignity as he could muster under the circumstances, he turned on the shower.

She joined him in mere seconds. "I can't believe I just said exactly what my mother would have said under the same circumstances," she said, not even noticing the magnitude of his manly pride. "Is that shower for me?"

"For both of us. Separation anxiety."

She gave him a look that said things might be happening elsewhere but they couldn't change what had happened between them. "I'll shower with you if you'll wash my hair."

"It's a deal. I'll wash every hair on your body."

While he gently massaged shampoo into Cecily's thick mane, he thought regretfully of how much fun this would be if he could take it slowly, lather every inch of her and then slide against her while she was wet and soapy. But Cecily, in spite of that look, seemed hell-bent on speed.

"Conditioner," she said tersely, and when he'd put it on and rinsed it out, she leaped out of the shower. Through the frosted glass he could see her body in motion, rapidly making progress toward getting ready.

More slowly than the situation warranted, Will rinsed off the last of Cecily's shampoo that clung to his body, thinking about her focus on the task at hand—in this case, her maid-of-honor responsibility to Sally—and wondering if that focus, that sense of responsibility, had any connection to her decision never to get married.

Could he ever convince her that he was the same kind of person and that two people with massive senses of responsibility were people who could love and understand each other and would do anything in their power to make the relationship work? Because a relationship was a big responsibility, too.

Could he do that? Did he want to?

Before he explored the internal mysteries of Cecily,

he had to deal with Gus, Sally and this fiasco of a wedding.

He stepped out of the shower to find Cecily's face hidden under a curtain of hair. Wearing the tiny cream-colored panties he'd picked out for her, with one foot propped up on the bathroom counter, she was peering out from under the curtain, polishing her toenails with her right hand and wielding the hair dryer with her left.

"A multitasker," he said approvingly, whipping out a razor and shaving cream.

"Damn. I don't know how anybody gets this stuff on without dribbling it over the edges," Cecily said grimly. "How likely is it anybody will look closely at my toes?"

"I will. In fact, I may give them some fairly close attention after dinner."

"Then you can repaint them when we get home if they offend your aesthetic sensibilities. I don't dare do more than one coat or they won't get dry." She put her feet on the floor and attacked her fingernails with polish.

Even Will—because he'd grown up with Muffy— knew things were getting dicey when Cecily attempted to polish her fingernails and dry her hair at the same time. "Let me help," he said, attempting to wrench the dryer out of her hand.

She struggled to hang on to it. "You have to get yourself ready."

"Hey, you're looking at Transformation Man. I can make myself acceptable in five minutes flat." He finally had a grip on the hair dryer, which he applied to the back of Cecily's head while she studiously, although not skillfully, applied polish to her fingernails.

"Sally said something interesting," she said from under her hair-shield. "She said, 'He promised me no more dangerous work. That's what the security company is all about—no more dangerous work.' That's why she's so hysterical. But what dangerous work? That's what you're looking for, Will. What was he doing before he set up his security company? Will! My hair needs drying, not my boobs."

Too stunned to aim properly, Will was hung up on the two words *dangerous work*. He'd seen Gus's bio— the neat, straight bio of a neat, straight man. So had Sally's father. This was a fact he had to keep secret forever. Mr. Shipley had had Gus investigated all the way back to his kindergarten days and had come up with the American dream of young and successful manhood. Nothing dangerous about the guy.

Except that this dream man had disappeared the day before his wedding.

On the bright side, Cecily had appeared the day before the wedding.

Will reaimed the hair dryer, tossing Cecily's hair with his fingertips, loving the heavy, silky feel of it. The bad always came along with the good. It meant he had to keep his brain compartmentalized, and thinking about it, he realized that compartmentalization was what people expected of accountants. If only accountants' private parts could be trained to get the message.

While he ruminated, Cecily had disappeared, then returned to the bathroom in the silk dress he'd picked out for her. Seeing it on her for the first time, he gave up his regret for the nachos. She was all he wanted to eat for as long as he could see into the future.

"You look fantastic," was the best he could manage. "I need my five minutes, and we're off to the rehearsal dinner."

"Separately," Cecily said. She put down the makeup brush she'd been wielding and looked at him, her gaze sliding over him in his black briefs, resulting in a disastrous effect on the fit of those briefs.

"Right. Of course. We'll reintroduce ourselves during the cocktail hour." *And I'll fall in lust all over again right there in front of everybody.* He thought about the two of them on the sofa mangling "America the Beautiful," how he'd relaxed into the strength he felt inside her. *So maybe there's a little more to this than lust.* "Right," he said again, quickly, grabbing for his dress shirt, turning away from her distracting eyes.

"GATOR, OLD MAN! SHE LET YOU come tonight. Here, I brought enough cigars to stink up the whole hotel." Will handed over a Sutherland's bag and shook Gator's hand vigorously. When that didn't feel as if it were enough to express his feelings, he put a hand on Gator's shoulder and gave it a squeeze.

He loved Gator. Redheaded, freckled, homely as a lizard, Gator was brilliant at business and adored Muffy. Will couldn't be happier that Muffy had made a good marriage—and moved to Waco.

"Thanks," Gator said, accepting the cigars. "I'll pay you back."

Will waved his hand dismissively, then moved in close. "We have problems," he said. "Gus is still AWOL."

"Oh, God," Gator groaned. "That explains why Sally's on her third martini."

Will checked his watch. "It's only eight-fifteen."

"Right. She's holding up great so far, though. Look

at her over there, smiling and blowing little air kisses. But I can imagine what she's thinking—that if this wedding falls through, everybody's going to say she shouldn't have given marriage a second go, especially with somebody she doesn't know anything about." Gator shook his head, then lifted it to gaze around the room. "Look at the money the Shipleys have poured into this wedding."

The smaller of the Courtland's two ballrooms was the venue for the rehearsal dinner. Round tables for eight were arranged toward the back of the room, sporting arrangements of white flowers that reached up toward the many crystal chandeliers. The men in their dark suits and the heavily iced women in their designer cocktail dresses were having drinks on the dance floor, while waitstaff wove among them with cold shrimp, smoked salmon canapés and small peppers stuffed with cream cheese.

Will snagged a pepper. "Whatever happens, it's an event Dallas won't ever forget. I know I won't."

The door to the banquet room opened, and it was as if a sudden breeze had wafted through the room. Cecily stepped in, ruffles dancing around her knees, her hair full and glorious, her face lightly made up, her legs bare and her sandals sexy. Every eye in the room was on her as she made her graceful way toward Sally, who was standing on a chair, apparently planning to climb up on a table, while Mrs. Shipley stood beneath her, obviously pleading.

"Oops," Gator said, "looks like Sally's cracked."

*Everybody's looking at Cecily, but I'm the only one who knows her toenail polish is sloppy.* Will had to clear his throat before he could speak. "Hey, Gator, that's the doctor who delivered your baby."

"My baby's godmother. Cecily," Gator said, going teary eyed and apparently forgetting all about Gus.

"Come on," Will said, thinking he'd better claim Cecily immediately, before some other guy took her away from him. "I'll introduce you."

"OH, CECILY, MY DEAR, YOU LOOK stunning." Looking and sounding surprised, Elaine Shipley fled the spectacle of Sally and rushed to Cecily's side, wringing her hands. "Sugar, would you please see if you can do something with Sally? She's crazy mad at Gus and about to make a fool of herself, and her Daddy's threatening murder. Not to murder Sally," she added unnecessarily, with more hand-wringing, "to murder Gus."

Cecily saw Jim Bob Shipley out of the corner of her eye. A gentleman rancher, Texas-tall, he was wearing an elegant, Italian-cut suit with cowboy boots, and while he'd taken off his Stetson, as was proper, he was hanging on to it tightly. That's how mad he was.

"Of course," Cecily said soothingly. "Really, Elaine, I'm sure Gus will show up any minute and everything will be fine. You and Jim Bob mingle, you know, keep down the rumors among the guests, and let me try to get Sally in order."

"Good luck," Elaine moaned as she skittered off to grab Jim Bob by the arm.

"Hi, Sally," Cecily said, looking up. "Sorry I'm late. Come down and let's talk."

Sally gave her a hard, wild look, then took her foot off the table she was about to climb onto and got down from the chair she was using as a ladder.

"What were you about to do on the table?" Cecily said. "Dance? Strip?"

"No, my dancing-on-tables-and-stripping days are over. I was about to make an announcement," Sally said.

"Announcing what?"

"That Gus hasn't jilted me. He's just late." Sally waved an unsteady hand around the room. "Look at this. Everybody's afraid to come over and say hello because they're so embarrassed for me that Gus isn't here." She turned to Cecily, tears in her eyes. "My own party, and nobody will talk to me."

"I'm talking to you," Cecily said, "and I know you're right. Gus hasn't jilted you." She put an arm around Sally. Sally's shoulders were tight with tension. "But if he has—"

"You think he has?"

"Of course not. I know he hasn't, but if he did…"

She was going to tell Sally this much—that if Gus had bolted, he wasn't worth marrying anyway. But her voice faded away, as did the room and everyone in it, at the sight of Will walking across the floor in his dark suit, crisp shirt and black tie. He looked strong and solid, and the remembered warmth of his skin, the erotic thrill of his caresses, the memory of him drying her hair and the way he'd run his fingers through it, sent heat flooding to her face even as the tenderness of that moment made her uneasy in her heart.

"Hey, Gator," Sally said to the red-haired man with Will. "Congratulations, Daddy. Thank God there are a few good men left in the world."

Gator gave Sally a quick kiss. "Have a cigar," he said. "I have a message for you from Muffy. The doctor says she can be in the wedding if she feels like it. Isn't that fantastic?"

With a quick spin he grabbed Cecily in a bear hug.

"And it's all because of this woman. How can I ever thank you?" he burbled onto the top of her head, going teary eyed again. "I'm so grateful you were there."

"It's my pleasure," Cecily puffed into Gator's suit jacket.

Will gently peeled Gator off Cecily. "I guess I don't need to do introductions after all. Lucky me." He took her hand and smiled at her, an earthquake-producing smile—the earthquake taking place in Cecily's knees. "Thanks again."

She couldn't stop looking at him.

Sally's attention had been momentarily distracted from her missing groom, but now she was focused again. "You two knew each other a long time ago, right? Crazy you got together again here. Will, have you heard from Gus recently?"

"No," Will said, still smiling at Cecily. But then he seemed to shake himself loose. He turned to Sally. "Gus is here, isn't he?" He was the very picture of innocence.

"No, he's not here," Sally said, bitterness showing up in her voice. "Why should he be? It's only his rehearsal dinner."

"Oh, my," Gator said, equally innocent.

"Where is he, Sally, and what is he doing?" Will said.

Cecily sent him a glance. He was wearing an interrogator's intense expression. She gave him a surreptitious poke with her elbow. "He called me," she said as if all three of them didn't know it already, "and said he had to go out of town this afternoon and please give Sally the message, but he didn't tell me where he was."

"Are his parents here?" Will said. "Or family members or friends? They might know." He clearly hadn't gotten the point of her elbow in his ribs.

"Gus has no parents. He has no family members. He has no friends as far as I can tell, except that scumbag pirate Derek who isn't here yet, either." Sally's voice rose. "Who have you ever known in your life who didn't have any family or friends? The topic never came up until we started on the wedding invitations. How was I to know? I need another drink." She snagged a member of the waitstaff. "Get me a vodka martini, straight up. No fruit. Fast."

Sally's tentative grip on composure was slipping fast, and Will wasn't making things better.

"What's up with that Derek, anyway?" she continued. "I thought the best man was supposed to look after the groom, make sure things like this didn't happen." She hiccuped.

If Sally didn't shape up, she wouldn't make her own wedding. On the other hand, it was possible she wouldn't have a wedding to make.

"We all need to remain calm," Gator said nervously.

"I am calm," Sally muttered. "It's the rest of you who're getting your panties in a twist."

"I'm going to have a glass of wine," Cecily said quickly. "Anybody else?"

"I'll get the wine," Will said. Cecily observed that Will looked conscience stricken for having tried to pump poor Sally for info in her time of trial. "White or red?"

"White," Cecily said.

"I'll help," Gator said.

"Wine drinkers," Sally said, slurring the words. "Whatever happened to real men?"

"THIS IS BIZARRE," GATOR muttered to Will while they waited at the bar. "Feels more like a wake than a rehearsal dinner." He grabbed a handful of mixed nuts, ate the cashews and offered Will the rest. Will took them. Anything for Gator.

"The doctor's a pretty little thing," Gator said next.

"Competent, too," Will said, wondering if Muffy had told him Cecily was in fact a veterinarian.

"She single?"

"Yes," Will said.

"Hmm," Gator said.

"Shut up," Will said. "I have enough problems already." And in fact he had a new one. A big one. Somebody had a killer grip on his elbow, right at the funny bone. He turned to see who it was. "Uncle Jim Bob," he said, trying not to squeak from the pain.

"What the hell's goin' on here, Will?" Jim Bob Shipley growled. "I'm sick of actin' like everything's fine when that sumbitch has gotten my baby all upset and turned Elaine into a blithering idiot."

"Have a drink, sir." Will extricated his elbow and discreetly rubbed it.

"Just what I was after. Bourbon and branch," Shipley said, interrupting Gator's order. "No, skip the water and make it a double. Congratulations, Gator. Good thing somebody here's happy."

"Have a cigar," Gator said.

Shipley took it and sniffed it. "Good cigar. Wish I could say the same thing about that sumbitch—"

"Your drink." Will handed it to him.

"I'm gonna kill him when I see him," Shipley said. "I'm really gonna kill him if I *don't* see him. I told Sally, I told her a million times, don't hook up with a man until you've met his family. That's what tells you about a man—his family." He upended the glass of bourbon and drank the two shots in one massive gulp, then handed the glass back to the bartender for a refill.

"I'll take Cecily's wine to her," Gator said, deserting Will.

Shipley grabbed Will's shoulders, squished them together and hissed into his ear. "There's something else, too."

"What?" Will said with the last breath in his collapsing lungs.

"Don Galloway. Somebody burglarized his room this afternoon."

"Congressman Galloway? Oh, my God," Will said. "What got stolen?"

Shipley frowned. "I don't know. But the whole thing was kinda strange. He went up to his room, and—"

"Jim Bob, darling, Mayor Watkins is here. Come say hello." Elaine Shipley tugged at her husband's elbow, and he followed her, as docile as a bull with a ring in his nose.

Will straightened his shoulders, took several deep breaths, then glanced at Cecily. This was his chance to get back to her. He wanted all these distractions to go away so he could get back to making love to her, do it right this time, give her a night she'd remember forever. He started in her direction, where she was still talking to Sally.

"Hey," Sally said, making a sloshy turn toward Cecily, "you and Will seem to be getting reacquainted pretty fast. Y'like the way he turned out?"

"He seems very nice," Cecily said.

"Will is nice," Sally said. "I wish he'd been my brother. Muffy doesn't deserve him. Now Will, wine drinker or not, is a real man. I thought Gus was one, too," she said grimly.

"Muffy's changed," Cecily said, steering the subject away from the groom. "I mean, not that I knew her before, but according to Will—and now you—she must have been..." She halted because Sally wasn't listening.

Her gaze had suddenly zeroed in on someone who'd just come through the ballroom doors. "Speaking of real men, there's Derek."

She was on the move, streaming across the room like a heat-seeking missile aimed at a darkly handsome man. As Cecily watched, Sally grabbed him by the arm and yelled loudly enough to carry halfway across the ballroom, "Where the hell is Gus?"

# 9

"IT'S UP TO US, BUDDY," WILL said to Gator, seeing Sally near the door yelling at Derek Stafford, Gus's best man. He set down his wineglass.

"To rescue Derek from Sally? I hardly know the guy." But Gator put his wineglass down, too.

"Nobody knows him. So nobody is going to rescue him but us."

"Does he deserve rescuing?"

"Well, I don't know," Will said. "It's Gus who deserted Sally. Derek's here."

"You have a point," Gator said. "But think how Sally's feeling. One husband gone already, public humiliation when that marriage ended, now Gus has disappeared. Even when Sally's feeling good about life I would pity the guy facing her wrath."

Will wondered if it were possible that Gator had never faced Muffy's wrath, or if he'd faced it and just hadn't noticed. "So we might just two-step over..."

"Real slow..." Gator added.

"...and run interference if we need to."

They were already on their way, cowboys to the rescue of a guy who looked as if he could take care of himself—with anybody except Sally on the warpath.

Will observed that Cecily had set off toward Sally.

The room was humming nervously. Elaine Shipley had her feet braced against the floor and was hanging on to Jim Bob, probably to keep him from turning a gracious and elegant rehearsal dinner into a barroom brawl.

As they crossed the room, they saw Derek put his hand on Sally's arm, saw that Sally had stopped yelling, saw her engaged in earnest conversation with the man.

"He must have said the magic word," Cecily said, suddenly at Will's side.

They sauntered up beside Sally and Derek. Sally said, smooth as cheesecake, "Derek, remember Will? And Gator? This is Cecily, my oldest friend and maid of honor."

Will shook hands, did and said the right things but was increasingly troubled for two reasons. One was his certainty that Derek and Sally knew where Gus was and were keeping it a secret. The other was the way Derek's hand reached out to Cecily, who took it and shook it. He knew that's what everybody did—proffered a hand and the other person took it—but in this case it was Cecily and a man who was way too good-looking. Plus, he had a dark and dangerous air about him that Will knew for a fact women just loved. No wonder Sally had called him a pirate.

Derek's smile was as thin and tense as his handshake was warm and lingering—at least, Will thought it was warm and lingering—when he was shaking hands with Cecily. "Sally and I were talking about Gus," he said. "I know I was supposed to keep him captive until we made it through the wedding, but who can control a guy like Gus?"

"Right. Who?" Sally said. She seemed to be listening intently to every word coming from Derek's mouth.

"Anyway, I just heard from him. Everything's fine, but he can't take off in this weather."

"There is no weather." Will narrowed his eyes. "It's just hot."

"The weather where he is," Sally said, school-teacher patient.

"Which is?"

Sally looked at Derek. "I guess it's okay to tell, isn't it?"

"Sure," Derek said. "One of the companies Gus does security for had a break-in. Gus had to investigate."

"But where—" Will said.

"While the crime scene was fresh," Sally cut in. "That's the kind of guy Gus is. Responsible. Thanks, Derek, for coming by to tell me."

"What company did you say he—" Gator said.

"Gus said he'd kill me if I didn't," Derek said. "Excuse me. I'm going to speak to a few people before dinner."

"Me, too," Sally said. "I want everyone to know Gus is all right."

"We can calm down and have a great dinner, with or without the groom," Derek added. "A few years from now, we'll all be laughing about this."

Left alone, Will and Gator gazed at each other for a long moment. "Did you believe him?" Gator said.

"Believe what? He didn't tell us anything."

Gator nodded. "Something fishy's going on."

"You have no idea," Will muttered. He couldn't confide in Gator, either, no matter how much he wanted to.

"I gotta leave you with it for a while, Will. I need to call Muffy and see if her milk's coming in all right."

Yeah, Gator wouldn't want to sit through the

evening without knowing that. Will hoped he'd understand a concern about breast milk one day. "Okay." He felt dull and tired. "I'll hold down the fort, but if you hear gunfire, cut the call short. And say hi to Muff for me. By the way, Gator…"

"Ummm?" Gator's mind was clearly on his baby's milk supply.

"Do you think Muffy's changed?"

"Oh, yeah. She's gained a lot of weight. Maybe, she'll lose it, maybe not. I'll still love her no matter what." With a wave, looking happy at the thought that he'd soon be talking to Muffy, Gator left Will alone with his thoughts.

Derek Stafford was smooth. Too smooth. Even now he was moving smoothly through the crowd with Cecily on one side and Sally on the other, acting like a man who thought he was all that.

Will glanced around the back of the room where the tables were and observed place cards at each table setting. He scanned the names on the cards, located his own name, then went looking for Cecily's. The wedding planner's staff had put her next to Derek. The maid of honor next to the best man. Well, to hell with that. He didn't care if the wedding planner had a stroke. He switched Cecily's card with the one to the right of his own spot.

Then he realized Derek wasn't even sitting by a bridesmaid anymore and someone might notice the error. So he looked around for another bridesmaid's card and put it beside Derek's, then went back to the spot where he'd picked up the bridesmaid's card and found she'd been sitting beside her husband. He went on a search for a different bridesmaid to sit beside Derek.

In no more than five minutes he'd pretty well messed up the tables. So be it. All that mattered to him was to have Cecily sitting beside him, and he'd achieved it.

A gong sounded, inviting the guests to sit down for dinner, so he began looking for Cecily. He couldn't find her. He moved through the crowd, trying not to look as frantic as he felt, sighting all the people she might have chosen to chat with—the Shipleys, the other bridesmaids now surrounding Sally, undoubtedly hearing the excellent news about Gus—without finding her.

Worse, he didn't see Derek, either. He became increasingly certain that she was somewhere with Stafford. A man with a mission, he strode out of the room and into the hallway, past sitting rooms and meeting rooms, checking each of them. A few people looked up, startled, but none of them was Cecily.

He started back the way he'd come and caught a glimpse of pale silk coming around a corner. "Cecily!"

"Will? Is something else wrong?"

"Where have you been?"

She gave him a look. "I went to the powder room."

"You were in the powder room with Stafford?" He'd have the man arrested.

"Of course not. Why would I be in the powder room with him?"

"That's what I'd like to know." He folded his arms over his chest. Inside, he was fuming, angry, hurt. Face it. He was jealous as all get out.

She moved closer to him. He could smell the soft scents of citrus soap, shampoo, baby powder, lotion—the simple scents of Cecily. They only made him feel worse.

"I haven't been anywhere with Derek Stafford." She looked up at him. "What made you think so? Have you lost your mind?"

He uncrossed his arms. "Maybe." He wrapped an arm around her shoulders, spun her away from the ballroom and into an empty sitting room, then kicked the door shut with his foot. "I've lost my cool, that's for sure."

He wanted her more than a man had a right to want a woman, wanted and needed her to ease the weight on his shoulders. It had tripped him, this burden of feeling responsible for fixing the crises swirling around him—Gus detained on some mysterious mission, Derek too smooth with his explanations, Sally too quick to believe whatever it was Derek had told her, Elaine Shipley with a wedding threatening to turn into a disaster. Tripped him so badly that thinking Cecily had left the room for a quick tête-à-tête with Derek Stafford had set off an explosion inside him.

She'd warned him, hadn't she, that sex for her was a series of one-night stands? The longer he saw her in action, the less he was able to believe her, but if it were true, he realized he wanted to be her entire series of one-night stands. He could do it. He was up to it. And he intended to demonstrate it.

His mouth closed over hers. It was like honeycomb against his, meltingly sweet, opening to him, inviting the invasion of his tongue. And he accepted the invitation, exploring, teasing, melding with her in a dance of deepening passion.

Her body felt wonderful against his, long and slim, all woman and filled with an energy that buzzed through him, stirring him to pull her closer, feel all of her melt against him. Her breasts moved against his chest and his hands slid downward, feeling the narrow waist yield to his pressure.

Her mouth slid away from his, making him feel sad. "Will…" She was breathless. "We have a rehearsal dinner still to get through."

"They can get through it without us." He slid his hands down her back, pressing her hard against him, relishing the feel of her moving against his erection. He didn't give a damn about Gus or Sally. He just wanted Cecily, wanted her desperately, wanted her now.

His fingers tugged at her dress, scrunching it up in his hands until he could feel the lace of her panties and closed his fingers over them instead, stroking her, sliding his hands under her. And then he lifted her off the floor. It was his private fantasy—and his chance to make it come true.

She gasped, then locked her thighs around him, just as he'd dreamed she would, rocking with him, meeting his thrusts, her head flung back in ecstasy. Until, very quickly, she cried out, collapsing against him, shuddering, her hair shrouding him in its silky strands.

He held her there for a moment, agonized by desire, wanting nothing more than to take her upstairs and reach that same peak, have that same release himself.

But…regretfully, he lowered Cecily to the floor and tucked her head against his cheek. Even aching with frustration, so hot he itched to get out of his skin, he remembered that he did indeed have a few little responsibilities in there—responsibilities to his family and a responsibility to learn as much about Gus as he could from anyone who might know the slightest detail about the man's life, especially about his business. He sighed.

"Will..." Cecily sounded as if she could be talked into shirking her responsibilities. But then she sighed, too. "You're terrific," she said simply and made things much worse by reaching up to kiss him lightly. "You've made me feel so good, and now I want to make you feel good, too. But..."

"Just what I was thinking. *But.*" He smoothed down her dress, stroked her hair back into submission, wiped a little smear of eye makeup off her cheek, then slowly, painfully, escorted her out the door and toward the ballroom.

He hoped he'd still fit under the table.

THEY WALKED IN TO A MILD level of chaos at the back of the ballroom. Guests darted about, bumping into waiters who were attempting to deliver first-course plates and pour wine. "I left my Judith Leiber bag where my place card was before," a bridesmaid said, "and it's not there anymore. Has anybody found a sparkly little frog on his plate?"

"Dr. Connaught!" The wedding planner, wearing peach again, flagged her down. "We've had a little mix-up. My assistant is certain she seated you beside Mr. Stafford, but it seems she accidentally put another bridesmaid there. She's already sitting down, I'm afraid. I could ask her to move...." Her eyes said she *so* didn't want to.

Will choked on a cough. "I'll find our seats," he said, moving swiftly away.

"I don't mind at all," Cecily said. "Don't worry about it."

"Hello, there, Paula Perry." A woman in a stunning black dress stalked up to the wedding planner brandishing a place card, her eyes blazing. "Well, you finally found a way to pay me back for not asking you to plan my wedding."

"What's the problem?" Paula Perry rolled her eyes.

"You seated me at the same table with my ex-husband and his twenty-two-year-old spandex bimbo, Kimmy, the Pilates instructor. Thanks *ever* so much. I'm sure we'll have a lovely talk about my flabby abs."

"Meredith, I would never do something so childish. I can't even keep track of your weddings." Ms. Perry seemed to be holding her own. "Someone did mention seeing a man back here looking at the place cards during the cocktail hour."

"Don't give me the suspicious-stranger-changing-the-placecards story. I know you—"

"I'll trade seats with you," Cecily interrupted her.

The woman gave her a not particularly friendly glance, and instead of "Thank you," said, "Where are you sitting?"

"I don't know yet."

"I'd better find your place and check out the table." She got Cecily's name, then, teetering on her four-inch heels, the woman stalked away.

"She's had several husbands," Ms. Perry explained, "and they're probably all here. If you'll excuse me, I see another crisis developing at table five."

The woman in black returned. "Okay," she said to Cecily, handing her a place card with Cecily's name written on it in calligraphy. "It's just Muffy's stuffy brother I'll have to sit by. Not the most exciting company in the world, but I don't mind him."

"Muffy's what?" Cecily was floored. She'd lucked into a seat beside Will and had given her rights away to this terrible judge of male flesh? No wonder Meredith's marriages hadn't lasted. She turned around to see Will several tables distant, standing behind his chair and looking shell shocked.

She marched over to the table, whisked up the Meredith Winslow place card and firmly stood her own in its place. "Sorry," she said, "I've changed my mind. I'll help you find another place."

The woman didn't seem to mind sitting beside Congressman Galloway, whose wife was on his other side. Galloway and his wife looked less than happy about the situation, but you couldn't please everybody. Feeling she'd done her best, she returned to Will.

"Sit down, Florence Nightingale," he said through his teeth.

She sat. He pushed in her chair and sat down beside her. While he spoke to an older woman on his left and the man to her right was talking with the woman on his right, Cecily watched Paula Perry soothing the guests, straightening things out, and knew she herself would have made a terrible wedding planner. She didn't even want a wedding of her own.

No, this was just the way she wanted it—sex with attractive men when she found them, and nothing more. She just needed to find them a little more often. No, a lot more often. She really needed to get serious about it. Finding Will again had been the purest stroke of luck. She thought about finding her next man and felt an unpleasant little ripple of distaste run through her stomach.

She turned to Will and found him gazing at her. She looked deep into his eyes. "It is sort of coincidental, isn't it, that we're sitting together?"

"As coincidences go," Will said, "it's a great one."

"Uh-huh," Cecily said. "You did it. You are the 'suspicious stranger' seen loitering around the tables."

"What?"

"Just a little gossip I heard."

"Want to know what the suspicious stranger was thinking?" His voice, deep and very soft, stroked her like a feather.

"I'm endlessly fascinated by the motives of suspicious strangers."

"That if you were sitting beside him, he could do this," Will said and put his hand on her knee, then ran it straight up her thigh to the cream-colored panties.

Cecily shifted in her chair, feeling her eyes close, stifling a moan. What did that woman Meredith mean, "Muffy's stuffy brother"? Will had behaved outrageously, if not downright lawlessly, since the minute he charged into St. Andrews. Could that have been mere hours ago? It seemed like a lifetime.

A waiter set a first course in front of her. It was an elaborate tower of endive, pears, walnuts and diced bits of crispy bacon. A salad erection. The thought brought a nervous giggle to her throat.

Will had been chatting politely with the woman to his left, and now that everyone at the table had been served, he dived into his erection—or rather his salad—with gusto.

He was left-handed. Had to be, although his right hand, still resting on Cecily's thigh, was equally skillful. Just when she'd forked a bite of salad into her mouth, she felt his fingers spread around the circumference, then felt his thumb on the most sensitive part of her.

"Ah-ahh," she said, half rising from her chair. "Great salad."

"WILL."

Will heard his name coming from across the table and decided he'd better get his hand off Cecily's leg, which he did as furtively as possible.

"Did you hear about Congressman Galloway's room being trashed?"

The question came from Max Mitchell, a college friend of Will's, who was sitting across the table with his pretty wife, Maggie.

"I heard it happened," Will said. "That's all. Did Don lose anything valuable?"

Max patted his mouth with his napkin, stood up and came around the table, where he hunkered down between Will and Cecily, making Will exceptionally glad he had both hands in full view. "It's a weird story," he said sotto voce to Will. "It'll probably be in the newspaper tomorrow, but can we keep it private for now? You know I'm one of Don's supporters, like your folks. I wouldn't tell anybody but you."

"Absolutely," Will said. He had to smother an inappropriate smile when he saw Cecily had stopped chewing, probably in order to eavesdrop.

"Well—" Max moved in even closer and lowered his voice even more. "Don checked into his room this morning. Nora wasn't going to join him until tonight, so he went out for lunch and did some errands, I guess, and when he got back to his room, his door was wide open and a housekeeper was in there screaming."

"My God. What had happened?" Will was getting an uneasy feeling.

"I heard—"

If Max tucked himself in any closer, he'd have his head in Will's lap like a large and affectionate dog.

"—that clothes were tossed all over the place. Not

his clothes, his sister's. I don't know why he had his sister's suitcase. Maybe she's coming in for the wedding and sent her suitcase ahead for Don to hang on to until she got here."

Will's heart skipped a few beats. "How do you know they were his sister's?"

"He told hotel security they were and then the police when they got there. The clothes were plus sizes for big women. You know Nora. She's about the size of a parking meter."

Will's gaze met Cecily's. She wasn't even pretending not to be listening. Her eyes were wide and her sexy mouth was open. She was thinking exactly what he was thinking, and she didn't even know Don Galloway. And he knew in his heart that she, like him, would never reveal what she suspected.

"Will?"

Will whipped his attention from Cecily back to Max.

"What do you think? Don's been a congressman for—what—six terms? You think somebody vandalized his room to see if they could find anything interesting for his next opponent to use against him?"

"Sounds like it," Will said. "Politics is nasty. And all the vandal managed was to mess up Don's sister's clothes."

"You know his sister?" Max sounded both interested and a little bit competitive. He knew Will's folks were on intimate terms with Galloway, and in politics this was a status symbol.

"Y'know, I'm not sure I've ever met her."

"One of those invisible political siblings," Max said. He gave Will a friendly jab to the shoulder and went back to Maggie.

Will went back to Cecily, feeling purposeful, and found the soft, sweet nub wet and waiting for his touch.

CECILY ENJOYED THE SALAD while her lower half enjoyed Will's artful thumb moving against it, keeping up the happy-diner-relishing-the-cuisine facade while she relished his touch. His thumb moved gently, rhythmically against her, and when he slipped his fingers inside her, she stifled her gasp.

She couldn't get enough of him. He'd just sent her sky-high in the sitting room, but she didn't seem to be coming down. It was unbearable, the pleasure of it, the heat and heaviness spiking to every nerve in her body. Her face felt hot, her lips swollen, and it became more and more difficult to keep up the pretense.

The sensations that threatened to take control of her demanded relief. So she moved with him while he stroked her, a wiggly sort of happy diner, while a torrential flood built up inside her, higher and higher....

"Ummm!" Conversation at their table ceased as all eyes focused on her, including Will's, which sparkled wickedly. "A chocolate tower," she breathed, gazing adoringly at the dessert the waiter had just placed in front of her while patting the mist of perspiration off her forehead. "My favorite."

She was looking at the second erection of the evening—no, the third. She attacked this one with a fork and sneaked her left hand onto Will's lap. Now it was her turn.

"You're right," he was saying to the woman on his left. "Dallas has to be constantly vigilant about reserving green spa-aces!" he said suddenly and a little too loudly when her fingers made contact with his swollen heat.

"Oh, look," she said sweetly. "It's time for the speeches, and, my goodness, Sally's up on the stage."

Sally was indeed on the stage, looking beautiful, her dark hair gleaming, her ivory sheath perfectly fitted, her pearl jewelry elegant and classic. Someone clinked a knife against a wineglass, and the hum of the room died down.

"Hi, everybody," Sally said with a big, wide smile. Her audience clapped, and she waved them regally into silence. "I know it's not the usual thing for the bride to make the first rehearsal-dinner speech, but these aren't the usual circumstances."

For a moment, the hum rose again, as if people were asking each other whether something embarrassing might be about to happen.

"I want to say a special thank you to everyone who *did* show up, unlike a *very* important member of the wedding party who did *not* show up." She said it with a giggle in her voice, and generated a nervous laugh from her guests. "In fact, what you're apt to remember about this wedding is the list of primary players who didn't show."

She mentioned Muffy and congratulated Gator's and Will's parents. "This special baby was delivered by none other than my very first friend and my maid of honor, Cecily Connaught, who is actually…" she paused, building up the interest, then said, "…who is actually a large-animal vet in Blue Hill, Vermont."

"What?"

Gator's cry of alarm rose above the laughter of the audience and had Cecily snatching her hand from Will's lap. He leaped up from his seat several tables away to stare at Cecily, his freckled face bright pink.

"Muffy didn't tell him," Cecily whispered to a

dazed-looking Will. Gator looked really mad. She wondered if he ever got violent. Or litigious. She'd prefer violent.

"I guess she didn't want to worry him." Will looked thoughtful as he gazed back at her, and she wondered what he was thinking about.

She looked back at Gator to find he'd joined in the laughter. What a relief.

Sally took back the floor. "The bride's father usually makes the first speech, but this bride's father is madder than a coon in a cage at this bride's groom, so I'm not letting him up here on this stage. Y'all know my daddy and what he's like when he's mad, and here he is, Jim Bob Shipley. Stand up, Daddy. And Mama, you stand up, too. My mama, folks, Elaine Shipley. Let's lift our glasses in a toast to Mama and Daddy for giving us a beautiful party tonight."

"Hear, hear," chorused the audience, standing for the toast.

Sally's speech went on and on. She introduced everyone in the room by name without making a single mistake and mentioned something personal about each of them. She smiled, she laughed and soon had everyone relaxed and in good humor. Cecily felt so proud of her.

At last, she brought out the pièce de résistance. "Now we're going to hear from Gus," she said, "and about time, don't you think?"

She waited for the laughter to die down, then said, "Gus dictated this to me on the phone." She slowly pulled out a piece of paper. "And asked me to read it to you tonight if he didn't make it." She paused, looking innocently around the room. "Gus, you here?

Guess not. Okay, here goes. 'You're gathered together, I'm stuck in the weather, you're wondering whether I'll make it at all. But I'll put on that tether if I have to burn leather, if it takes my last breath, or die trying. 'Bye, y'all."

The poem had a familiar ring about it, imperfectly rhythmed and perfectly dreadful. Just like the poem Sally would read to Gus in lieu of the traditional vows—if Gus made it to the wedding. In the midst of the applause, Cecily turned to Will and found, as she always did, that he was already looking at her. "Gus didn't write that poem, Sally did," she whispered.

"She's lying about everything," he whispered back. "But I have to say this for her, she's a trooper."

He reached for his wineglass. Cecily reached for hers. "Let's do it," she said, realizing she was once again about to do exactly what her mother would have done in these same circumstances.

"We'd like to make a toast," she called out, "to Sally!"

# 10

"IT WAS A PLEASURE SITTING with you," Cecily said, holding out her hand to Will.

"For me, too." With a smile, he took her hand, stroking the back of it with his thumb and not letting go.

The man should patent his thumbs. That gentle caress and the gold gleam of his eyes were a dangerous combination. But soon they'd be alone and she could handle all the danger he wanted to get her into.

"I'm sorry to see the evening end," he said.

Revelers surrounded them, and Cecily was unwilling to share their secret with anyone. "It does seem a shame. So," she said, extricating her hand before she lost her cool and jumped him, "I'll just say my goodbyes and thank-yous. I look forward to seeing you tomorrow at the wedding."

"If not sooner." His eyes flickered at her.

"I look forward to that." She fled while it was still possible.

She looked around for Gator, hoping to give him a chance to bawl her out for being a veterinarian, and found him in a corner talking on his cell with a finger stuck in his other ear. He was laughing. Good sign. When he saw her, he took his finger out of his ear, blew her a kiss and gave her a thumbs-up sign.

She smiled back and went in search of Elaine and Jim Bob Shipley.

On the way she saw Sally surrounded by the rest of her bridesmaids. She didn't look as perky as she had while giving her uplifting speech. Her mood seemed to be darkening. She'd put on a terrific public show, but she wasn't happy about what Gus was doing. Cecily bit her lip, wishing the wedding weekend were going more smoothly.

Spying Jim Bob, she thanked his scowly face for a lovely evening, apologized again that her parents couldn't arrive until the next day, then found Mrs. Shipley.

"Oh, Cecily, honey, I just wanted to make sure you'd hung up your dress for the wedding. If it's wrinkled, you'll want to send it out for pressing." She patted Cecily's arm. "Your mama would never forgive me if I let you come down the aisle wrinkled, but I must say, seeing you tonight, I think she greatly exaggerates your tendency to ignore your appearance."

Prickles shot up Cecily's neck, and they had nothing to do with this latest shot from her mother. The problem was that she hadn't given the slightest thought to her maid-of-honor outfit. "Don't worry about a thing," she said as her heart began to thud. What she knew for a fact was that her suitcase was a mess. And as for the dress—it was in the suitcase, wasn't it? She'd covered it in plastic and then…

It was the *and then* part that was giving her neck the prickles.

"Samantha, of course, is one of those never-a-hair-out-of-place people," Elaine Shipley went on. "When you were a baby, she kept you the same way—always perfect, never a spot of dirt on you."

*No wonder I chose to fill my life with cow dung.* "Thank you again, Elaine," she said as she fled, panicky, to the elevators.

WILL SMILED AS HE WATCHED Cecily take off at a run. She was as excited about the night they'd spend together as he was. He'd take his time going up, let her pretty herself up, get into that skimpy gown—

Maybe he wouldn't take his time.

Still, there were people to speak to, an alarming number of whom had heard the story about Congressman Don Galloway. He didn't know what was going on, but damn it, Galloway was an old friend and he didn't want him libeled or Nora hurt.

He'd corroborate Don's story about his sister's plus-size clothes no matter what Don was up to.

He sought out Max Mitchell first. "I just remembered, I may have met Don's sister once," he told him. "She lives in…Australia, I think. Owns a sheep ranch in the outback, so she's rarely here. A big woman, almost as big as Don."

"Somebody told me she wasn't coming for the wedding," Will told another friend, who shared the story in absolute confidence. "She came back to Dallas to attend to some legal matters, so when she got to the hotel, she asked Don to hang on to her suitcase while she saw lawyers. That's what I heard, anyway."

He'd almost reached the doors of the ballroom when Elaine Shipley rushed up to him. "Will, I feel so sorry for Don's sister, Wilma, having all her things messed with. If I can do anything for her… I have a special saleslady at Sutherland's and I bet they'd open up for her early tomorrow morning…."

Ah. The congressman's sister had a name now, and it sounded as if one of the gossips along the way had named her after him. No one would remember that the rest of the information about Wilma had come from Will Murchison.

Congratulating himself, Will started for the elevator bank. He hoped he had enough condoms. A practical man—and a hopeful one—he never traveled without them, but Cecily might test the number he'd arrived at based on his earlier experiences.

Not Cecily herself, but the way he felt about Cecily. It was a warming thought, and when he reached the seventh floor, he sped like a rescuing knight to his room.

He walked in to find a covered tray loaded with cold nachos and fajitas, the grease congealing over them, and not two but four bottles of warm beer. Lovely. A midnight snack. He put the tray under lamplight, which would at least melt the visible grease, then went back out and down to the ice machine, dumped the ice in the bathroom sink, buried the beer in the cubes and laid a bath towel over the arrangement. It wasn't champagne and caviar, but he was a man in a hurry and the last thing he wanted was a waiter coming to the door.

And while he'd been engaged in his culinary preparations, he'd dreamed up another little surprise for Cecily. A few minutes later, he opened both doors with a flourish and delivered a vocal rendition of the trumpet signal that the walls of Jericho were falling. What he saw stopped him cold.

Cecily was circling the room, fully dressed, with clothing littering the bed. Her suitcase was there, too, upside down. She'd even dumped her medical bag.

When she looked at him, her eyes were enormous, intensely blue and wild.

"I can't find it," she wailed.

Will had to push his left brain to the max to come up with an adequate response. "Your diaphragm? Your sponges? Not to worry. I have condoms, and the firm requires a blood test every three months. Until further notice I'm free of all known diseases—"

"Not birth control. My dress. I can't find my dress."

"You're wearing it." She'd flipped out. Was she allergic to something they'd had for dinner? Nuts? Chocolate?

"Not this dress." She grabbed a handful of the silky, ruffled dress he'd picked out for her, lifted it and shook it at him like a flamenco dancer, then dropped it. "My maid-of-honor dress." She sank down on the bed and buried her head in her hands, her hair flowing forward to cover her face. Then she looked up and her eyes widened. "Will, you're buck naked."

True. He was. That had been his surprise for Cecily—to go to her room without the clothes she'd accused him of being neurotically attached to, indicating that he'd put Gus on the back burner and was ready to give her a night of quality time. Now it seemed it hadn't been such a great idea. "Hang on," he said, went back to his room and returned in the wildly printed boxer shorts he liked to sleep in. "Let's start over," he said. "What do you mean you can't find the dress? A long white dress—" he was sure it was white, and furthermore, several different kinds of white "—isn't the kind of thing you can lose. The earrings, maybe, or the little white gloves—"

"It's not lost. I know exactly where it is," she moaned, hiding her face again.

"And..."

"It's in Vermont. I forgot to pack it."

"Oh, God," Will said, sat down beside her and buried *his* head in his hands. They sat there in silence for a minute or so.

"How can we fix it?" Will finally roused himself to say. He also had the presence of mind to put his arm around Cecily. Just because he obviously wasn't getting laid until he found Cecily's dress didn't mean he couldn't try to comfort her in her crisis.

"There...is...no...way...to...fix...it." She sounded like an old-fashioned record on the wrong speed.

"There is always a way." He gave her a little squeeze, then got up to pace the room, which was supposed to help you think. "Somebody could FedEx it to you."

"The last FedEx pickup at the general store was at seven o'clock. Josh Miller's our FedEx man and he's so dependable. I know because I send out specimens to—".

"You could wear my tux shirt and tights. Sometimes the maid of honor has a different getup from the bridesmaids, doesn't she?"

She looked at him. "Not *that* different."

"Where'd the dress come from? Maybe the store has a spare."

"They're Vera Wang, custom made. Mrs. Ogletree in the Ben Franklin fabric department measured me and I sent the measurements to Sally and Sally shipped the dress to me for a final fitting, but it felt okay to me just as it was, maybe a little loose in the waist, and Mrs. Ogletree offered to take it in, but I said loose was better than tight and it was fine as it was and now it's in my closet in Blue Hill." Another wail rose from low in her throat.

"Somebody could fly down with it tomorrow morning."

"I can't ask Moira to do that. Besides, she has to take care of my cats."

"Who's Moira?"

"Dr. Vaughn's and my new resident. Just out of the Iowa State vet school, excellent credentials and she's turned out to be even better than we'd hoped. She offered to stay over while I was gone. She's also a very nice and cooperative person who has a real grasp of what it means to work as a team—"

"How many cats?"

"Eleven, but I've only been working there three years."

Will's depression was deepening, but he forced himself to concentrate on Cecily's problem. One of them had to. She was finding her solace in stream-of-consciousness babbling.

"Some of the dairy farmers don't treat their barn cats right. They don't do anything to keep them from having babies, but when they do, they…destroy the litter." Her voice broke in a sob. "Dr. Vaughn and his wife had the full responsibility for taking in the kittens until I got there and volunteered to take half."

"How many cats do the Vaughns have?" Will whispered and realized with a not unpleasant little shock that he was imagining himself living with a squadron of killer cats.

"The number holds pretty steady at around thirty," Cecily said. "But it's okay. The Vaughns built the cats their own house."

"Built the cats their own—" Will stopped himself. The information coming in was more than he could process when he had so many other things on his mind. "Cecily, try to focus on the dress. We can talk about feline rights later." *And about us.*

"Oh. Right. The dress." She flung herself backward against the pile of clothes on the bedspread. "All is lost. Sally should never have asked me to be her maid of honor. My mother should have known better than to make me accept. Maid of honoring isn't one of my skill sets. Packing isn't one of my skill sets, either."

"Didn't you say your parents were flying down here early tomorrow morning?" She looked so accessible, stretched out on the bed, it took all the practicality he could muster to get the question out.

"Break of dawn. How else could they get here by noon?" She got up and began to unload the bed. Will observed that she put some things in dresser drawers and others in the trash can. He hoped she'd be happy with her choices later. "Mother's in a bad mood about it, I can tell you that, and it's all because of the paper Daddy had to give in Chicago that she'll probably have to put on her makeup in the limousine and dress for the wedding at four in the morning, but do you think she'd come without him? No-oh. Ohhhh." She was back to wailing again. "She's going to be so mad at me."

Feeling dizzy, Will closed his eyes tight and opened them again. A family dynamic, one for which he was sadly lacking in data, was going on here, so he'd have to look at the bottom line and hope he'd guessed right. "I was wondering if she'd bring you the dress."

Cecily's body went very still and she opened her eyes. "How's she going to get it?"

"Well…" How the hell did he know? "Somehow we have to get the dress from Vermont to New York. Where in New York?"

"Manhattan. Greenwich Village."

Will felt another wail coming and didn't know what had set Cecily off this time but felt certain he'd find out. "Could they drive up to get the dress?"

"It's a six-hour drive from the Village to Blue Hill. It would be five if Daddy had gone to Columbia instead of NYU, but we can't base our professional choices on my ultimate convenience, can we? Especially not the convenience of a daughter who was dumb enough to forget her maid-of-honor dress. Anyway, how could he have known that he needed to work somewhere closer to northern Vermont?"

Will stuck to the point. "Six hours down, six hours back." She was right. All was lost. He decided he'd go ahead and order champagne and brandy and they could both get schnockered to forget their sorrows, but when he looked back at her, she'd sat up and she had a weird light in her eyes.

She stared into space for a moment. "I can't do it," she said. She'd emptied the bed, and she flung herself down on it again.

"What?"

"Ask my mother."

"Sure you can." He wasn't sure where this was going. The wedding was in thirteen hours. It wasn't possible to make a twelve-hour drive and make the wedding in thirteen.

"No, I can't." She sat up again. "But I have to. And I have to ask Moira if she'd be willing to meet them halfway. She'd be within her rights to file suit with the, the…oh, whatever the agency is that protects employees from having to drive through the night on errands that have nothing to do with their job descriptions."

As Will started to answer, the phone rang in his room. He was weighing his choices—answer it, don't answer it—when Cecily said, "Answer it. I'll keep thinking."

*About what*, he wondered, *your cats?* But he went into his room and picked up the phone.

"Will. Gator."

"Hey, Gator." Will picked up a cold nacho and took a bite. Not bad. "Everything okay?" he said with his mouth full.

"I just wanted to know if you heard the news about Don Galloway. He was holding a suitcase for his sister—you know, Wilma? With the safari operation in Ghana? And—"

"I heard," Will said, smiling to himself. "Tough, huh? Listen, Gator, I've been talking to Cecily—"

"You have?" A curious note crept into Gator's voice.

"Yes," Will said firmly. "She's on the other line and I need to get back to her. She has a big problem. She forgot her dress for the wedding. It's in Vermont, a million miles away from here, so we have to figure out—"

"Hang on," Gator said. In a minute he came back to the phone. "Muffy says Cecily can wear her dress and she'll skip the wedding. It'll be too big, but Muffy says there's a way to pin it so it'll fit."

Muffy? Willing to miss being in the wedding, and all because she wanted to help Cecily out? "I'm touched," Will said. And he really was. "Muffy would do something like that for Cecily?"

"There's nothing we wouldn't do for that woman."

"Hold the phone a minute and I'll tell Cecily," Will said, rushing it before Gator could get emotional again.

He crept across the floor and into Cecily's room, where he found her sitting on the bed, staring into space.

"Good news," he whispered, pointing to his room and putting an imaginary phone to his ear to indicate that the phone was still live. "You can wear Muffy's dress."

He expected excitement. Instead Cecily said, "I wouldn't dream of doing that to Muffy. You're Sally's cousins, and it sounds to me as if you two have always been close to her. Muffy was willing to haul herself up out of bed twenty-four hours after having a baby—that's how important Sally's wedding is to her. She has to be there."

"But—"

"I'm not backing down. Far better for Muffy to be in the wedding."

Defeated, Will slunk back into his own room.

"She won't do it," he told Gator. "She insists it's more important to Muffy than to her."

"Well, okay then," Gator said cheerfully, "we move on to plan B."

"Which is?" Will frowned.

"She can take my plane to Vermont and get the dress."

"Gator!"

"Why not? Like I said, we'd do anything for that woman. It's a matter of a couple of phone calls. I'll get back to you in a few minutes."

"Cecily," Will yelled when he'd hung up, "deliverance is on the way."

"Oh, good," came a listless voice from the next room.

He stepped in. "Something about the situation is upsetting you a lot more than it should. I mean, it's upsetting you to the point of making you dysfunctional. I mean that in a nice way," he added quickly.

"That's me. Dysfunctional Cecily."

"No, no, no, what I meant was…"

"It's true. I've reached the point that I can only function in one area—veterinary medicine. I'm an *idiot savant*." Already slumped, she slumped even more.

Will took off his tie. "We'll talk about it on the plane."

"What plane?"

The phone rang. Will went for it.

"It's all set," Gator said. "The pilot's on his way to the field to file a flight plan. They're gassing up the plane and doing the inspections. He says be there in an hour."

"Gator, have I ever told you that the day you became my brother-in-law was the happiest day of my life?" Will said, and rang off.

He was afraid the blunt statement that they were flying to Vermont to get her dress would put her over the edge. He'd better lead up to it slowly. "Cecily," he said, "Gator has thought of a way to get your dress."

She looked up at him. It was progress.

"He has a plane."

Her eyes flickered slightly.

"He's loaning it to us."

Her face lit up. "I can flee the country and escape total humiliation and my mother's scorn."

"No, we can go to Vermont to get your dress. He says the plane will be ready to leave in an hour."

It finally registered. He could tell because she leaped up. "I can't believe this," she said. "I can't believe Gator's doing this wonderful thing." Then after a second or two of glowing, she got down to business. "Let's see, it's eleven-fifteen. An hour to the airport, four hours to Vermont, an hour to Blue Hill, an hour back, four hours back to Dallas—what time will that be?"

"Ten-fifteen tomorrow morning."

She drooped a little. "That's cutting it pretty close. And things happen, delays..." She lit up again. "But if Moira would meet us at the Burlington airport with the dress, that would cut off two hours."

"I wanted to see where you live. I wanted to count cats."

"But what if—"

He gave in. "You're right. Call her. I'll pack a couple of toothbrushes for us."

"Will, you don't have to go with me. You shouldn't go with me. In fact, I'll have to insist you let me go alone. What if something happens and you miss the wedding, too?"

SHE GAZED AT HIM, wondering what she'd done right in her life to be given a second chance to know him. She'd offered him a one-night stand and had mainly delivered frustration and chaos, in return for which he'd given her passion, affection and one-hundred-percent support.

"You should be here, trying to figure out what Gus is up to."

"I'll take my laptop along. I'm going with you." His eyes darkened and his face showed an unexpected bit of uncertainty. "Unless you don't want me to."

"I want you to," she whispered. Then she burst out, "This isn't fair to you, not any of it. We were supposed to be in bed, me being as good to you as you've been to me, and instead we'll be on a plane—"

The uncertainty on his face was gone. "In the back of the plane is a berthable sofa—it turns into a three-quarter bed. There's a double-lined privacy curtain between the bed and the cockpit, and the bathroom's in the front of the plane. Pilot and copilot in the front, us in the back behind curtains." He gave her a slow, suggestive smile. "For the first time since my beloved sister Muffy went into labor I'll have you alone. I wouldn't miss this flight for anything in the world." He licked his lips.

Cecily was close to drooling, and had been since he mentioned the bed. "We'll be killing two birds with one stone."

He pulled her into his arms and gave her a promising kiss. "Speak for yourself. I'm not all that easy to kill."

She threw her arms around him. "When should we leave for Love Field?"

He consulted his watch. "Twenty minutes."

"I'll call Moira." She dialed her home phone number.

Moira picked up right away. "Cecily. Hey, are you having a good time? The babies are doing great. We had tuna fish for dinner."

Moira was so nice. She was smart *and* nice and clearly wide awake, probably studying. "I would be having a good time if I hadn't forgotten my maid-of-honor dress. Moira, could you, would you…"

Moira could and would. Except…

"Of course. Bring the usual cats with you. Will

wanted to see them anyway," Cecily assured her. "You'll find a stack of carriers in the basement next to the boiler."

"Who's Will?"

"That's a long story. For later."

The arrangement made, Cecily gazed at the phone for a while, then picked it up and phoned her parents' apartment.

"Cecily! Are you all right?" Her mother's voice was sleep-clogged.

"No. I have something to tell you."

"You're in the hospital. You're fatally wounded. You're—"

"No, just feeling humble."

The silence began to alarm her. "You really aren't all right," her mother said at last. "Sugar pie, I'll call our psychiatrist friend in Dallas—"

"No need, Mother. I called to tell you I understand at last why you were always after me to keep my clothes in order and to think about events I'd be attending while I was packing for a trip. I apologize for slamming my door in your face when you came to my room to ask if I'd packed skin toner to take to the university. I'm sorry I yelled at you when you sent the box of nude pantyhose after your one visit to me in Blue Hill. I deeply regret the call I made after you sent the makeup. I've used it twice already today."

There was another silence and then her mother said, "Something is terribly wrong."

"Or terribly right."

"Don't do anything foolish until I get there tomorrow."

"Have I ever done anything foolish? 'Bye, Mother."

Had she ever done anything foolish? Not until now.

Feeling good about the call, Cecily looked around to see what Will was doing. He'd assembled a little pile of things he thought they'd need and was staring at the pile, eating a nacho. "Have one," he said.

"Thanks. They're cold," she said after taking a bite.

"I noticed. I've got your toothbrush here and some other stuff, like shampoo, just in case."

"I have to take my medical bag."

"Of course. We'll pack this stuff in it." He roused himself. "Let's go."

THE ENGINES THROBBED BENEATH them, matching the throbbing of Cecily's heart. Several minutes to take-off, Will motioned her into the rear of the plane, where he'd already pulled out the sofa. "This is what I dreamed of doing when I saw this dress on the mannequin," he said, sliding his arms around her.

"What?" She didn't have to ask. She could feel the answer in the way his hands slid across the thin silk, caressing her skin with the fabric, sliding down her spine, sending a shiver of pure pleasure straight through the center of her body.

His hands cupped her buttocks, bunching up the silk, then smoothing it out, sliding under her to lift her up to him. He teased the ruffle down the front with his knee, opening the dress, tugging her tightly against him. She moaned against his shoulder, feeling the strength of his need, reveling in the sheer largeness of him, imagining him encompassing her with his arms, imagining herself encompassing him with her thighs and at last taking that pulsing part of him inside her.

"Ready for takeoff." The voice that came over the intercom system was dry—no Hollywood training here—and the message was unwelcome. Slowly Cecily disentangled herself from Will's embrace and led him back to the seats in the front of the plane, where they sat side by side on luxurious leather and dutifully buckled up.

They sat in silence, then Cecily met Will's sidelong glance with her own. "I have plans for you," Will said and stretched out his legs.

"What plans?"

"When that seat-belt sign goes off, I'm going to jump you."

Cecily giggled. "Surely you can be a little more inventive than that."

"Um. Maybe I can." He took her hand, threaded his fingers through hers and slid them back and forth.

It hit Cecily that they'd never held hands before. There was so much she didn't know, hadn't experienced with Will. They'd never gone to a movie, discussed a book, cooked something together. This realization forced her to face up to how short a time they'd spent together. So why did she feel so close to him? Was it because of their history in the long-distant past?

The sensitive skin between her fingers tingled at his touch. She felt like a teenager again, recognizing that first flush of desire. "Tell me what inventive things you're going to do."

"I'm going to nibble on your earlobes," he said and fastened his teeth on the one nearest him. "And then I'm going to blow in your ear, like this...."

A flash of heat went spinning from that small caress to the tips of Cecily's toes. With a roar, the plane took off—or was she the one who was taking off?

"And then," he said, "I'll chew your arm like a drumstick." His mouth settled on her bare shoulder.

She leaned into him, breathless, when his teeth barely grazed her skin, and then slid down the inside of her arm. When he reached the inside of her elbow, she moaned and slid down in her seat, her legs apart.

She felt his face buried between her breasts, felt his hand begin the slow trip from her knee to her thigh and simply put her arms around him and held on. His hair, silky against her skin, smelled clean and woodsy. She closed her eyes and rubbed her cheeks against it while he touched her in her most secret place. He nuzzled her breasts, his mouth open and wet against them, moving with excruciating slowness, tantalizing her, arousing every nerve ending in her body.

"We're cruising at twenty-four-thousand feet. You guys can relax now."

Cecily moved just in time to keep Will's head from decking her jaw.

"Come on," he said. His voice was low and husky. Together they returned to the back of the plane, and Will gazed at her as he closed the curtains tightly.

He came toward her slowly, touched her shoulders, her arms, ran his hands down her sides all the way to the hem of her dress, pulling it up an inch at a time until it covered her face, and holding it there, he brushed kisses down her breasts, her waist, her stomach, before pulling it off entirely. Gently he placed her on the berth and gazed at her while he unbuttoned his shirt, unzipped his trousers and at last was as naked as she.

For the first time she could have more than a glimpse of him, and she drank in his beauty and strength, his darkly glistening skin, the gold in his eyes glowing in the dim light of the cabin. Carefully he lay down beside her and stroked her, kissed her lips, her cheeks, her forehead. She had to touch him, and so she did, the skin of his penis satiny under her fingertips, the shaft rigid and ready.

His kisses deepened and a new urgency infused his caresses. Her desire exploded, matching his suddenly frantic need. He spread her legs and buried his face between them, flaming her with more of his generous kisses, his moisture mingling with the wetness of her. One touch of his tongue to her tiny, aching nub and she was already coming in deep, even spasms, each one an earthquake shattering her body. "Please," she begged him. "Please…"

He lifted himself above her and deftly applied a condom. Poised over her, hot, breathing hard and obviously at the end of his self-control, he hesitated.

She couldn't let it happen. "Will…" she said, tugging at his waist. "What's wrong? Why…"

He relaxed a little beneath her desperate hands and she heard his soft laugh, almost a sob. "I can't believe it," he said, smiling into her hair. "I keep waiting for the phone, the knock on the door, the pilots to tell us to go back to our seats, buckle up and put our heads between our knees…."

"Then hurry," she demanded. "It might happen." And she tugged at him with all her strength.

And then he was inside her, the massive length and breadth of him thrusting deeply, bringing with each thrust such exquisite pleasure that she cried out, her folds blossoming in his heat, opening up to him. She lifted her hips and wrapped her legs around him to pull him in even tighter. He gasped with pleasure, his thrusts growing more forceful, withdrawing only to plunge into her again ever more powerfully, until he drew her into a dream that was nothing but sensation, a sensation that ebbed and flowed, built and relaxed only to climb even higher.

At last the pleasure was too great and there was no holding back. With one last desperate thrust, he groaned and collapsed against her, carrying her along with him in wave after wave of shuddering delight, sliding his arms beneath her to hold her sweat-slicked body tight against his while she trembled in the aftermath of the most momentous, most fulfilling event of her life.

Tears of relief streamed down her face. It was not the right time to make a sensible decision. Even in her uplifted state she knew that. But what went through her head was that she didn't want to do this ever again with anyone but Will.

The thought terrified her.

# 11

"THAT WAS AS GOOD AS IT GETS." Lying by her side, Will ran a fingertip down Cecily's cheek.

They'd made love again, but this time she wasn't crying. This time they'd taken it more slowly, more deliberately, and it had felt dangerously more like love than sex. Looking up into his eyes, she wished she hadn't come to the wedding after all. Meeting Will had rattled the foundations of her life goals. A one-night stand had turned into a lifetime problem. *Keep it light.* "Where do you suppose we are?" Wanting to touch him, too, she traced his smile.

"We've crossed the Mississippi and we're over—" he squinted "—Tennessee. We're about half-way there."

"How do you know?"

"I'm looking at that little television screen behind you."

"Do you wear contacts?"

"No."

"Glasses?"

"No. You?"

"Not yet."

"Why did you ask?"

"You squinted to see the screen." Cecily yawned and stretched her arms over her head. The bed was barely big enough for the two of them—barely big enough for Will—and her hip overlapped with his, a nice feeling.

"Your hair was in the way."

"My hair is always in the way. Maybe I should cut it."

"Touch it and die."

She rested her head on her arm to gaze at him. Feeling very shy, she said, "I guess the real reason I asked is that now I know one more thing about you. I think—" she hesitated, wondering if this was a good idea "—we've sort of gotten to be friends again, don't you?"

He smoothed her tangled hair back from her face. "More than friends. We've been through a lot together since noon yesterday."

"It hasn't been the usual one-night stand," Cecily agreed. It might have been her imagination, but she felt him draw away from her a little—not his body, not his hands that still touched her, but something inside him. She wished she hadn't said it. It wasn't as if she'd had any one-night stands. How did she know what the usual one was like?

"A little more time and we might be best friends," was all he said.

"We have a little more time now," she said, stroking his chest, tangling her fingertips in the crisp, curly hair, tracing the triangle down to his waist and below. *Just not enough,* she thought.

"Hey, folks, time to wake up. We're thirty minutes from landing. We'll be asking you to get back into those seat belts in fifteen."

"Better timing than we've had in the past," Will

said. Reluctant to move at all, he untangled his and Cecily's arms and legs, got up and started pulling on his clothes. "I'm making a trip to the head. We have a small disposal problem."

"Not so small," Cecily said, gathering up condom wrappers from the floor. "You go first. I'll get dressed and straighten up the bed."

"Wonder what you do with these things on a plane?"

"Your guess is as good as mine. I've never done this on a plane."

He was glad to hear it. More or less dressed, he went forward to the rest room behind the cockpit. Once there, he saw a discreet, handwritten sign on the trash bin. Condom Disposal, it said.

Will stared at it for a long moment. Busted. The pilots knew exactly what he and Cecily had been up to beyond those drawn curtains. Gator must have tipped them off to the possibility.

He splashed his face with water. He never got away with anything. Muffy? She got away with everything—sometimes with his help, of course. He thought about other friends and acquaintances who seemed to have some magic going for them, something that let them come out on top, whatever happened. Not him.

He drew a line of toothpaste on his brush. Wasn't that the thing that kept him honest? The sure and certain knowledge that if he ever stepped out of line he'd end up in jail without passing Go and without collecting two hundred dollars?

And then he thought, *It's not the worst neurosis a guy could have.*

Except now, when it seemed likely that Gus's situation would force him to choose between professional ethics and family obligations.

On the way back, he'd talk to Cecily about it. He finished up in the rest room and returned to the back of the plane, where he found her dressed and sitting on the neatly made berth with her long, beautiful legs crossed and one sandal swinging. As soon as she glimpsed him coming back, she scampered forward toward the bathroom. "Don't let the plane go down without me," she said.

"MOIRA!" CECILY RAN ACROSS the tarmac and threw her arms around a plump, pretty, dark-haired woman dressed in jeans and a plaid shirt.

"Aren't you freezing?" Moira said.

"Yes. Thanks for asking." Cecily smiled at her.

"Here's a sweater." Moira draped a fuzzy blue one over her shoulders.

"Oh, fabulous. This is Will, Moira."

"Will Murchison." He shook her hand. "It was great of you to bring the dress."

"It was great of you to fly up with Cecily." Her smile was sweet and genuine, but it contained a certain speculative quality, too. Will knew that look. He'd seen it a million times. It was a woman-thinking-wedding kind of look.

"How's everything at the clinic?" Cecily asked Moira.

"Oh, just fine, except—"

"The pilots said they needed thirty minutes on the ground," Will said. "You two talk. I'll get the dress out of the car and put it on the plane."

"Thanks," Cecily said. "Now, Moira, what's the 'except'?"

Will walked toward a Subaru station wagon, the only car on the tarmac in the private section of the Burlington airport, and peered through the windows. On the back seat were three animal carriers but no dress. It must be in the trunk.

His curiosity got the best of him. He opened the back door and looked inside the window of one of the carriers.

"Mrrr." A small black paw touched his nose through the window.

Will thought that was really cute. "Hey, kitten. Got some friends in those other nylon palaces?" It was cold here, a sharp contrast to the heat of May in Dallas. He'd be warmer in the car, so he climbed in, pushed the cases over to make room and sat down before he looked through the window of the second carrier, where an enormous yellow tabby was sitting up with its tail curling around its feet, purring at him. In the third case was another kitten, a calico. In a few minutes, the entire car seemed to be purring.

It was a comfortable sound. Will opened the two kittens' cases, then let out the big tabby. An outraged "Meow" came from the front seat, where, upon investigating, Will found another case and opened it. A fluffy gray-and-white cat got out, stretched and leaped straight over the seat and onto his shoulder.

He was covered with cats. They not only purred, they snuggled, climbed, kneaded him with their soft paws and very sharp claws. He leaned back and closed his eyes.

"Will." Will jolted awake. It was Cecily, looking at him through the car window, which he rolled down an inch. "What are you doing?" Her voice softened.

"Hey, Buster. Look, Mommy's back for a minute. Come on, Rags, give me a snuzzle." Both cat and woman put their faces to the crack.

Will yawned. "I thought there were eleven of them."

"These four love to ride in the car. They would have been heartbroken if Moira had left them at home."

"Thirteen," Moira said from behind Cecily. "You have thirteen cats."

"Don't be silly, Moira. I only have eleven."

"Thirteen. I counted."

"When I left at four this morning," Cecily said pointedly, "I had eleven."

"When I got to your house at seven," Moira said firmly, "you had thirteen."

Cecily stared at her. "Somebody brought home friends?"

"Apparently."

"Huh," Cecily said, then turned back to Will. "Have you had a good time here in the car with four of my *thirteen* cats?"

"Yes." It surprised him, too. "They almost put me to sleep."

"So I noticed. We have to put them back in the cases so Moira can take off. The pilots are calling us. You got the dress, right?"

"Wrong," Will said, struggling to convince the calico it wanted back in its case.

"Will! What if we'd let Moira drive away with it because you decided to organize a little predawn playgroup?"

"I don't know. We'd have to come back, I guess." He'd put everyone away now, and while they weren't happy about it, they seemed to be settling down. He got out of the car, opened the trunk and got the dress. "Back to our chariot. Thanks again, Moira. Glad I got to meet you."

He got the same speculative look in return, but this one was a little more positive. "Great to meet you, too." She smiled. "Safe trip."

"I DIDN'T KNOW CATS WERE SO…relaxing," Will said.

The sun was coming up and the sky was streaked with pink as the plane took off to wing them back to Dallas. The mountains were a hazy blue, the trees bare-limbed with a few touches of bright, new green at the tips.

"You folks want some coffee when we level out, there's a carafe in the kitchen area with some cinnamon rolls. Water, soft drinks, snacks—help yourselves."

The voice came over the intercom. The pilots had apparently decided invisibility was the safest route with these two passengers.

"Coffee?" Cecily said.

"I was thinking about a little more, um, sleep," Will said, putting his hand on her knee and caressing it.

An hour and a half later, bone-tired and satisfied, Cecily fell asleep, then woke up to an odd clicking sound. She rolled over. Will wasn't in sight. He must have moved to the front of the cabin. She slipped her dress over her head and peeked through the curtains.

Will sat in a booth composed of two long, leather-covered benches with a table between them. He'd plugged his laptop into the airplane's phone line and was frowning deeply and scrolling madly down a Web page. A cup of coffee and a huge cinnamon roll sat on the table. He was up for the night.

With a deep sigh, she faced up to the truth. She'd

hoped Will was a playboy who'd take her out of herself, and instead he was a workaholic just like herself.

Barefoot, she snuggled in beside him on one of the padded benches and put her head on his shoulder. "Okay," she said, "let's see what we can learn about Gus."

"IF HE'S TELLING THE TRUTH—that the weather is keeping him away—he must be in the D.C. area," Will said a while later. "I talked to the pilot just before you woke up. He said we took a half circle around the area to avoid the storm, and according to the Internet, Dulles and Reagan airports are the only ones showing canceled flights due to inability to take off. The other airports, like O'Hare, are just suffering the consequences, waiting for planes out of D.C., people missing connections, that kind of thing."

"What could he be doing there?" Cecily wondered aloud. "Planning to blow up something?"

Will leaned back and shrugged. "Steal something? Make a big drug delivery?"

"Now we're catastrophizing."

"He has income coming from somewhere."

"What are you going to do?"

"I don't know. I don't have enough evidence to stop the wedding. I don't have any evidence, just suspicions."

"You have to make your suspicions known sometime, though, don't you?"

"I was hoping I could just ask Gus outright and tell him he has to prove anything he tells me before I can file his tax return. I'd rather do it after the wedding—if there is a wedding."

"And let Sally marry a dangerous man?"

Will hesitated. "Didn't you get the feeling that Sally and Derek were in on whatever Gus is doing?"

"I did," Cecily admitted.

"So I'm not that worried about Sally anymore, unless Gus doesn't turn up for the wedding. I just wonder what I'm supposed to do." He laid his head back and closed his eyes. "Pursue Gus's sources of income down to the last dime, even if it means ruining him? And by doing that, making Sally unhappy, being resented by my aunt and uncle, damaging my mother's relationship with her sister, not to mention causing tension among our friends? Or just drop it, take Gus's facts as he gave them to me and sign the return?"

Cecily thought about it and knew it would be a hard choice and that the choice he made would reveal the kind of man Will really was. "The important thing," she said slowly, "is to make a choice. Whatever you do, do it all the way."

"Black-and-white. Family and friends on one hand, my profession on the other."

"I know. Hardest choice in the world." She paused, thinking. "Back in the old days, doctors often had to choose between saving the mother or the baby. There wasn't a halfway measure. There were so many things to take into consideration, like which one had the best chance of survival after the choice was made. Sometimes," she added, caressing him with her gaze, "they chose wrong, but they had to make a decision."

He sighed. "You're right. So do I."

"The sooner the better."

He turned to her, then picked up her hand. "Thank you. It won't be easy, whatever I do. But it would be easier," he said, looking deep into her eyes, "if I had you to help me through it."

"I'll be happy to talk to you anytime," she assured him. Inside, tension was building. She knew tomorrow couldn't end just like that with her going away and never seeing him again. They'd made too strong a connection—exactly what she hadn't intended to let happen.

"As you said, we've gotten to be friends. I want to be more than that."

"We barely know each other." She wanted to plead with him to go back to bed and stop all the serious talk. It would be a cop-out, but that's exactly what she wanted to do. Cop out. "There are all sorts of things you don't know about me. You might hate me when you got to know me better."

"I doubt that. But we'll never know if we're not together." He smiled a warm, sweet smile, that almost made her want to throw her arms around him and shout, "Marry me!"

But she didn't intend to marry. She was doing well in her field. She might practice a few more years and then start teaching in one of the schools of veterinary medicine. That would mean moving. To keep her options open, she had to stay free and unencumbered.

Even as all these sensible thoughts went through her head, she was getting drawn into the green-and-gold pools of Will's eyes. Her body was beginning to tingle. She was beginning to want him.

Oh, so much more than that. She was beginning to want to settle down with him and eleven—no, thirteen—cats. She had to shake the image and shake it fast. So she said the coldest thing she could think of. "Now, Will," she said with a bright smile and a sad heart, "you know this is just a little fling we're having, making up for the fling we didn't have when we were teenagers. It turned out to be more stressful than we'd planned, but we can't let our emotions run away with us and try to turn it into something it isn't."

He stroked her hand, started to speak a couple of times, then finally said, "Cecily, why wouldn't you let me kiss you that afternoon in the groundskeeper's cottage?"

She gazed at him for a long moment. "Because the staff were absolutely forbidden to become involved with the riders. The job at the stables meant a lot to me. If you'd kissed me, I would have been fired."

"The job meant more to you than kissing me?" She felt he was trying for a teasing tone, but he failed. He was asking her something deeper and more important.

"Whether it did or not, I'd taken the job and made the commitment," she said.

"But did it matter more?"

She couldn't look him in the eyes anymore. Gazing at the tabletop, she said, "I guess it did."

"Do you still feel the same way—that the job is more important than a personal relationship?"

"I don't know," she whispered. "I'm asking myself the same question."

She could tell he didn't like her answer, but he didn't let go of her hand.

HE UNDERSTOOD WHAT SHE WAS saying and instinctively he felt pain. In the few hours they'd spent together, exploring the physical side of their youthful friendship at last, he'd found something both gentle and tough as steel, sensitive and creative but smart and practical, as well. He wanted to do more exploring, wanted to give this relationship a chance.

Look at her—thirteen cats, four of who came to meet her at the airport. It amused him, but it also said something important about her. She was serious about her profession and he appreciated that. He was serious about his profession, too, but he wanted more than that one thing in his life. She had more love to give than casual sex would ever allow her to demonstrate. Their brief time together hadn't been one of many one-night stands for her, it had been a one-time thing. He was sure of it.

He surely felt like a man in love, and it was possible, of course, that she hadn't fallen for him the way he'd apparently fallen for her. That would hurt. Even if it hurt, he didn't intend to let her slip away from him without finding out.

"I didn't mean to scare you," he said, realizing he had. "I just think we ought to work out ways to see each other."

"Maybe we could do that," Cecily said, but her eyes were still round and worried. "Like a trip now and then. I do stay awfully busy, even on weekends…."

He waved that away. "So do I, especially in personal and corporate tax seasons, but let's say we manage it. After a few visits back and forth, if we're still liking each other—" he paused to smile tentatively "—you could look around at some of the cattle operations here, find out what veterinarians they use, see if you might like to work in Texas."

It alarmed him when her eyes narrowed. "You could see what accounting firms have offices in Burlington, too," she said.

"Yes, of course," he said in a hurry, then realized he should point out the negatives of his being the one to move. "In the accounting business, you usually do better in the long run by staying with the same firm."

"And you want to make as much money as you possibly can, for the cars and the clothes with logos."

"The what?"

"Nothing."

"I'll investigate Burlington, of course," he said, wondering what he'd said wrong.

SO THAT WAS THE BOTTOM line. Will wasn't impulsive enough to ask her this soon to give up her job for him, but he was suggesting that she would be the one to adjust to his job. She had no doubt she could find a position near Houston—one with a long commute, probably, but people adjusted to those long commutes. The closest veterinary school, though, if she followed through on her desire to teach, was in College Station, some distance from Houston. So she had a hard choice to make, too—stick with her career plans or do whatever it took to continue this thing she'd found with Will, whatever it turned out to be. It wasn't life and death, but it wasn't an easy choice, either.

If she let up on her career in order to spend time with Will and the relationship didn't live up to its promise, she'd have to work hard to regain her position in the veterinary world. If she stuck to her current attitude of total commitment to career and gave up the possibility of exploring a long-term relationship with Will she might regret it for the rest of her life. Her career was highly satisfying, but it wouldn't keep her warm at night or give her children or someone with whom to grow old. If she wanted those things, she'd have to reconsider her bias against marriage.

"We're tired and strung out, and I've given up on Gus for now," Will said. "We can talk some more tomorrow." He broke the awkward mood entirely by moving his mouth slowly down to hers and brushing it back and forth. "We're still more than an hour away from Dallas. Why waste a second of the time worrying about the future?"

No, not an easy choice. She opted for the physical delight of making love with Will, storing up for the dry season to come, and the plane roared on toward Dallas, the wedding and the time she would have to make that choice.

# 12

"GO UP TO YOUR ROOM and start ironing your dress,"
Will said when the taxi pulled up in front of the hotel.
"I'll take care of the driver." Cecily draped the dress
over her arm and started toward the entrance, but
he tugged her back. "After I check with Gator, see if
Gus has turned up, we can shower together—" he
dropped a kiss on her nose "—for old times' sake."

This was nothing like the old times. Looking back
at the way she'd yearned for Will, too shy to speak
to him, the way she'd run from her one chance to kiss
him, those times seemed a lot simpler. In her room,
she got out of her rumpled silk dress and gave it one
last pat before she stuffed it into her suitcase. How,
she wondered, did you get something dry-cleaned in
Blue Hill? She put on her blue-striped shirt and went
to the closet for the iron and ironing board. The dress
would challenge her domestic skills to the max.

She was already challenged long before getting to
the ironing part. It seemed that setting up an ironing
board was far more complicated than setting an
equine bone. It didn't surprise her to hear a knock on
the door to the hall just when she'd gotten herself ob-
scenely tangled up with the thing. As Will had said,
everything they set out to do seemed to be interrupted by a knock or a ring.

"Mother!" Samantha Connaught was the last person she'd expected to see when she opened the door. But there she was, standing in the hall, slim as always and beautifully clothed as always—but her hair was untidy, she wasn't wearing any makeup and she was leaning on a contraption that looked like a stand from which an intravenous liquid dripped into the vein of a hospital patient. "What happened to you?"

"What happened to me? After you called, I stayed awake the rest of the night wondering what had gone wrong. And now that I've seen you, I know my premonitions were right. You haven't even started getting ready, and you're supposed to be downstairs at eleven. Oh, dear, were you getting ready to *iron* your bridesmaid's dress?"

She bustled into the room in her pale blue silk suit and a second later she screamed. "Look at it!" She was staring at the dress that Cecily had laid out on the bed—the bed she hadn't slept in last night. "It's a wreck. It's supposed to be on the van going to the church at ten-thirty! Thank goodness I'm here. I'll get you ready and then see what I can do about my own appearance."

To Cecily's relief, her mother disengaged herself from the device she'd been hanging on to. No bags of fluid hung from it. There were no needles in her mother's still-shapely arm. "What the hell is that thing?" Cecily asked.

"Don't swear. It's my clothes steamer."

"You brought a steamer on the plane?"

"I called the hotel," Samantha Connaught said, sounding defensive, "and asked if the cleaning service worked on weekends. The very nice lady I spoke with said no, but there were irons in the room. Then

I started having nightmares about you ironing your dress, so I got Fred and me an even earlier flight on another airline and put us in first class. They were happy to put the steamer in the coat compartment."

"Mo-ther," Cecily groaned.

"You sound like your daddy. I ordered coffee and pastries for us. They should be up in a minute," Samantha went on briskly. "I was desperate for more coffee, and I know we shouldn't be eating pastries, but to heck with it, we are. I'll start steaming your dress. Get in the shower. You look like you've been up all night."

"That's what a wedding weekend is—party, party, party," Cecily said limply.

"Seems more like a funeral from what I've heard," Samantha said, unpacking equipment and examining the dress she'd laid out on the bed.

Cecily's eyes widened. "You know about Gus?"

"Elaine called me right after you did. She's hysterical. Jim Bob didn't buy the story Sally was telling at the rehearsal dinner, so he was storming around the house, calling private eyes on his cell while she and I talked. He won't have his little girl humiliated. He's decided to find the man and force him to go through with the wedding even if they have to do a quiet annulment in a week or two. She did tell me how pretty you looked last night. That was a relief. But the two of you left me wide awake and thinking I'd better get down here fast."

"So forget me and go to Elaine's rescue."

"Like you don't need rescuing? You have bags under your eyes. Thirty, with bags under your eyes." Samantha shook her head, then began searching for an electrical outlet for the steamer. "Go on, dear, take your shower. Why are you dancing around in circles?"

She was dancing around in circles in an attempt to keep her mother's back turned toward Will's room. For good reason. While her mother was bent double, her trim, blue-silk rear end jutting up into the air as she plugged in the steamer, the connecting door opened. Will stood there for a split second, the doorway framing him in all his naked glory, while Cecily pointed desperately toward the prominent rear end. He stared at her, frozen with shock, then silently closed the door.

She was thirty years old and realizing that nothing had changed since they were teenagers—he still made her want what she couldn't, wouldn't have. Their last chance to be alone together, to resolve the things they'd talked about in the night, had been stolen from them by an overzealous mother and a full-size professional clothes steamer.

She could think of only one thing to do—take her shower, and keep it cool.

"Now we'll do your hair," her mother said when Cecily had emerged from the bathroom wrapped in a towel. She frowned. "And your makeup."

"Mother, I can do—"

"Put something on first. Something cute and casual to wear in the limo."

"Yes, ma'am. Is that the coffee?" She pointed toward a napkin-covered silver tray.

"Get dressed. I'll pour."

Cecily cut the tags off one of the skirt-and-top combinations the Sutherland's salesperson had selected for her and went back to the bathroom with the outfit and the lingerie she'd wear under her dress. She slipped into the skirt. The top was a shelf-bra camisole. "Do I need a bra with the bridesmaid dress?" she called out to her mother.

Ominous hissing sounds came from steamer in the bedroom. "Of course you need a...well, no, I guess you don't. This thing has bones."

Cecily smiled and struggled into the camisole. It was pale blue. The skirt fit snugly over her tummy, then exploded into pleats, not too full, just flirty. It was cream with blue flowers. Why were people always picking out blue for her? It was pretty, though, and resembled the outfits the other bridesmaids had been wearing yesterday. She'd feel anonymous, and found the idea comforting. She felt that if anyone took a moment to look at her, they'd be able to read her like a book and know she was a woman reluctantly and despairingly in love.

Combing out her hair, she went back into the bedroom. Her mother had poured two cups of coffee, and Cecily picked one up. It was hot and fragrant. A frosted roll caught her eye, and she balanced it on the saucer. If only she could dispel the image of Will in her doorway, the memory of his hands on her in the night, she might actually feel faintly happy. All she could think about was that she'd never experience those moments again.

"I'll let this hang a while," Samantha was saying, "and then touch it up. Vera Wang was such a good choice for the bridesmaids' dresses. Now, let's get started on your hair."

Cecily suddenly felt tired enough to give in. She collapsed into the chair that pulled up to the desk while Samantha unplugged the steamer and plugged in her own hair dryer. When the warm air from the dryer hit her scalp and her mother began lifting strands of hair with a large, round bristle brush, Cecily felt a calm descend over her.

It made her feel like a little girl again, being dressed up for a birthday party. Her hair had been silvery-blond then, and everyone told her how pretty she was. Samantha had been a good mother in those days, tender and caring. It was Cecily herself who'd caused the problems between them. The very fact that her mother had named her Cecily indicated certain expectations, and they didn't include horses, gymnastics and veterinary medicine. Samantha had wanted a doll to dress.

Cecily pondered this and decided she could be a doll to dress for a few minutes, as long as it didn't impact the rest of her life.

"Your hair is so lovely. Will you wear it up or down?" Samantha's voice had softened, as if she, too, were reliving those days long ago.

"Sally has hairdressers coming to the church to do some kind of messy ponytail thing."

"I know the style."

"Mother…" Cecily had wanted to ask the question for years, and had a feeling the time was now—or wait for her own wedding day, which she was still fairly certain would be never. "What made you stick with Daddy instead of your career?"

Samantha aimed the dryer at the hairbrush wound with Cecily's hair. "I guess you're old enough for us to talk about these things."

Cecily hoped she was. She steeled herself against some terrible revelation that would change her perception of her parents forever. She took a sip of coffee, fortifying herself.

"The truth is…" Samantha said hesitantly, then she sighed. "The truth is, well, he's just fantastic in bed."

Cecily choked on the coffee, which went up her

nose. "Are we still talking about Daddy?" she sputtered.

"Of course," Samantha said, patting drops of coffee off Cecily's camisole with a damp cloth. "Who else would I be talking about?"

"But he's so quiet and reserved. He doesn't listen to you, he doesn't answer you...."

"That's when he's working." Samantha's smile was positively smug. "He's different at night. And in the morning. Sometimes at noon. We wanted more children, but I think the reason I didn't get pregnant again was that we made love so often that his sperm count was always low, so..."

"Mother," Cecily said faintly, "can we wait until I'm ten years older to expand on the details?"

"Of course. I don't want to embarrass you."

"It's too late. You have."

Samantha sighed. "I worried about you all through high school, looking for signs of nymphomania. Coming from the two of us, it seemed likely, but you didn't seem to inherit—"

"Yes," Cecily said distinctly, "I did."

It startled her mother, who would obviously have loved to ask for clarification, so while she was still looking gobsmacked, Cecily went into the bathroom and began putting on her makeup. Alone. She felt pretty gobsmacked herself. Her mother, *her mother*, had married for love and sex, had given up a career for love and sex. That was more amazing than learning that her reserved, studious father was in fact a rampaging tiger in the bedroom.

Amazing and in fact, just what she'd needed to hear at this important moment in her life.

Ten minutes later she was still working on her

eyes. She was doing it by the book—concealer, shadow, dark stuff beneath the bone, liner above and below, mascara and eyebrow pencil, resenting every instruction on that list the makeup salesperson had made for her mother. She looked at herself in a mirror and decided she'd met clowns who were made up more subtly.

But the worst was over. She checked the list for what she still had to do. Foundation, powder, blusher, lip fix, lip liner, lipstick, blotted, with lip gloss on top. She gritted her teeth. Maybe the worst wasn't quite over yet.

She was examining the row of brushes, looking for the one suitable for applying foundation, when she heard voices coming from the bedroom. Recognizing Will's, she went right out.

"Oh. Will. Hello," she said in a bright, unnatural voice. "Mother, this is…"

"We've been talking," Samantha said. Her eyes were gleaming almost lustfully. Not lusting for Will, lusting for this highly desirable male to be interested in her daughter. "I remember Will's mom and dad from long ago. We were just discussing the cruise through Alaska they're planning this summer."

"Yes, we were," Will said. His eyes were glinting with restrained mischief as he stood there in perfectly pressed khaki trousers and a black shirt with the sleeves rolled up, holding the hanger of a plastic-covered white suit, his groomsman gear. The suit would have done Elvis proud. "I was just telling your mother that Sally asked me to come by and see if you were ready. And also to carry your dress down for you."

Damn him, he was enjoying himself.

"Aren't you an *angel*," Samantha cooed. Cecily could hear her thinking, *What a well-brought-up young man.*

"Is Gus back?" she asked abruptly.

The fun went out of Will's eyes as his gaze slid from her to her mother. "Mother knows he left," she explained. "Elaine Shipley called her. Jim Bob didn't buy the weather story. He was calling private eyes, Elaine was calling Mother." That was interesting, too—that Elaine Shipley, with all her Dallas friends, would call Samantha instead, who she actually saw about twice a year.

"Last Gator heard, which was five minutes ago, he hadn't shown up yet."

Cecily groaned. "Sally must be at the end of her rope."

"Well, we all have to go on to the last possible second as though nothing were wrong," Samantha said firmly. "Stay positive for Sally's sake. And Elaine's. Cecily…"

When Samantha turned back to Cecily, Will's gaze skimmed up and down Cecily's skirt and camisole and he gave her a thumbs-up. Her mother was looking at her, but Cecily couldn't take her eyes off Will. Sally's wedding was falling apart, and she still couldn't think about anything but Will.

"…you're almost ready, aren't you, darling?" Samantha persisted. "Need any help with the rest of your face?"

"No," she stammered, trying hard to meet her mother's eyes, "I think I've got the hang of it. Go on downstairs, Will. I can carry my dress. It weighs about eight inches. I mean ounces." Heat rose to her face.

"Her dress is ready," Samantha said, "but why don't you wait for Cecily? You and I can visit while she does those last few little things."

"I need a bag with pantyhose and my shoes…."

"I've put that together for you. I'm sorry I didn't think to bring you a pretty little tote to carry, but…"

"Not to worry. Put everything in my medical bag."

"Your medical bag!"

"She never travels without it," Will said. His eyes were glimmering a little again.

"Yes, in my medical bag," Cecily said, giving Will a sharp look. "I'll hurry."

"And what happened to your shoes, young lady? I cleaned them up as well as I could, but…"

"I delivered a baby in them," Cecily said, whisking off to the bathroom.

"You what?"

"Let Will tell you," she yelled back. "It was his baby."

That ought to keep her mother from inquiring about inherited diseases or scandalous behavior in Will's family history—at least in the time it would take Cecily to finish giving herself the perfect maid-of-honor face, whatever that was. The wedding photos would be beautiful, even if the groom didn't appear in any of them.

"ALL RIGHT, DARLING, YOU LOOK wonderful and I'm off to do something with my face and hair." Samantha gave Cecily an excessively careful kiss and Will a little hug. "I'm so glad we met," she told him. "I'll make a point of seeing your mom and dad and congratulating Gator. Cecily, don't you dare leave the reception without telling us, okay?"

Will felt a stab in the pit of his stomach at this reminder that Cecily would be leaving soon, leaving without him, leaving without their having a moment alone together. "'Bye, Mother," Cecily was saying. "Thanks." A serious look came over her face. "You gave me something to think about." Then she was herself again. "Come on, Will. I've made us five minutes late. Sally's already upset enough. We shouldn't make it worse."

After his near miss, almost walking in naked on Samantha Connaught, Will had had a brainstorm. He'd thought of a solution to both his problems—Gus and Cecily. It would take some maneuvering. He might have to play hardball. But first he had to know if she wanted more of him than a few weekend visits.

They got on the elevator with several members of the wedding party, making it impossible for him to say anything with the bridesmaids making eyes at him, telling Cecily how gorgeous she looked and then lapsing back to the only topic of interest currently circulating through the Courtland—whether Gus had gotten back yet.

They got off the elevator to find Paula Perry, the wedding planner, hopping up and down on one stiletto heel and then the other. "Come on, wedding party, we need those outfits for the van. We have to load the limos." She was hustling them along, a dynamo in the same dress she'd been wearing the night before—the same color, anyway. A color a lot like Cecily's little top and bikini panties. *Dangerous thought. Drop it now.* "We have to get there early for the photographs. Move, move…that's it, suits and dresses to the van, then the men to the black limo and the women to the white."

They wouldn't be talking on the way to the church, either.

"Have you heard if Gus is back?" the chirpy bridesmaid asked Paula.

"He will be," she said, her lips set in a grim line.

Will fumed. He could rebel. He could accuse the wedding planner of sexist attitudes and demand to ride with the women. No, that wouldn't work. They wouldn't be alone. They'd be with all those women. Including Muffy, and then it would all be out in the open and his folks would be naming his and Cecily's first baby. So he'd demand to take Cecily in his car, no matter what anybody thought....

Unfortunately, while he planned his strategy, he'd somehow lined up with everyone at the van and then gone with the herd to the black car. By the time he'd decided what to do, he was sitting in the middle seat of the stretch limo, hot, frustrated and already missing Cecily.

He tried to imagine how much he'd be missing her tomorrow or a week from now. It was not a pretty thought.

# 13

AFTER A LOOK AROUND FOR WILL, Cecily got into the white limo. The three bridesmaids filled the back seat, so Cecily slid into the middle seat. Sally sat in the front, pale but beautiful, calm but not cheerful. Once Cecily was settled, she put her arms around her. "It's going to be all right. I'm sure of it," she lied.

"Of course it will," Sally said, sounding like a robot.

The limo door opened and Muffy got in. Cecily scooted over. Muffy said, "Cecily, you look beautiful!" and then threw her arms around Sally. "Don't worry, sugar, Gus will get here in time."

"Everybody stop hugging me and telling me everything's going to be fine," Sally burst out. "You're doing it because you know it won't be fine. Well, I know it will."

Her outburst was startling and they rode silently to the church. From the limo they went to a classroom-turned-dressing room, accompanied by the wedding planner. Mrs. Shipley waited for them there, wringing her hands, naturally. A hairdresser stood poised behind a chair, armed with combs, brushes and hair spray. Where there should have been laughter and joy, Cecily expected someone to say, "Scalpel, Nurse."

"YOU GUYS LOOK GREAT." THE speaker, a male assistant to the wedding planner, made a small adjustment to one of Will's shirt ruffles. "Just hang here until we call you."

"Why?" Will said.

The man blinked. "Well, the men are supposed to stay in here and the ladies in their own dressing room. Those are my instructions. We don't want anybody disappearing. Anybody *else* disappearing," he amended himself.

"I need to speak with one of the ladies," Will said.

"You can't go in there." The man was very firm. "No peeking."

"You're thinking about the bride and groom," Will argued. "The groom's not supposed to see the bride in her wedding gown until the wedding." He wondered if Gus would get to see Sally in her wedding gown at all. "Doesn't mean the rest of the wedding party can't see each other."

"All I know is—"

"Besides..." Will knew he was getting wound up, but he couldn't stop himself. "Besides, we're doing group photos before the wedding and we'll be peeking then. Why not now?"

He had the guy looking pretty nervous. Mutiny in the groomsmen's dressing room. Big stuff. "I'll find out," he said and scurried out.

Will left right behind him, bolting out into the hall of what appeared to be the educational wing of the church. He threw open every closed door in the vicinity and finally just bellowed, "Cecily."

No one answered.

A prim-looking woman passed by. "Happen to know where the bridesmaids are?" he asked her.

"No peeking," she scolded him.

So he followed her. The woman held a bag and had what looked like a pincushion around her wrist, and he knew for a fact that Muffy's matron-of-honor dress needed to be pinned. Will Murchison, sleuth.

Her path led him to the second floor of the wing, where he did his bellowing act again. "Cecily!"

A door popped open and Cecily's head popped out. "Will! They're holding us prisoner in here."

She stopped him dead in his tracks. "Cecily," he said in a hushed voice, "you look great in that dress." The way it hugged her breasts, she had no business being in a church. "Rapunzel, let down your hair?" he said hopefully.

"I would if I could, but I can't. The woman over there—" she cocked a thumb at the busy hairdresser "—just put it up and she'd kill me if I took it down. She used so much hair spray, I'm not sure it will ever come down," she muttered to herself. "But…" She came all the way out of the room and said, "I can escape."

She floated over to him, a butterfly in the white dress, elegant in long white gloves. He opened his arms to her. She came slowly toward him. His heart thudded in his chest.

Commotion suddenly filled the hall. "Okay, we're starting the photo shoot. Ladies, down to the chapel."

"Will, what are you doing here?" Muffy said as the bridesmaids exploded from their dressing room. Will swam with the sea of white as it trooped down the stairs and along a corridor that connected the wing to the church. He tried to stick close to Cecily, but in the corridor, Muffy tackled him.

"Will, I have something to say to you."

"Later, Muff."

"No, now."

They'd reached the chapel and apparently had a moment of free time while the photographer adjusted his equipment. "Now" was his time to talk to Cecily, maybe his only chance. Frustrated and impatient, Will tried to give Muffy his full attention.

"Thank you," she said, putting her hand on his arm, "for taking care of me yesterday. No one could have a more wonderful twin brother than you."

At last she had his attention. "Well, that's a first."

She smiled at him. "I know I was bad to you when we were kids, but..." Her smile faded. "I was always so jealous of you." She sighed. "I was the oldest twin, but you turned out to be the smartest and the nicest and the cutest and the most athletic—well, just *everything*."

He stared at her. Damn, were those tears stinging his eyes? He was falling apart!

"I wish I hadn't been such a bitch," she said, and her eyes shone as if she were about to cry, too. "I feel as if I missed out on the best friendship I could ever have had. Can we be friends now?"

*Can we do it quickly?* went through Will's mind as he hugged her carefully, mindful of the dress. This wedding, someone else's wedding, was turning out to be the beginning of the rest of his life.

As soon as Muffy had turned away, giving him one last smile and pat on the arm, he spun and found Cecily gazing wistfully at him. He went straight to her. "Cecily, we need to—"

"We're ready, folks. Okay, we want to start with a shot of all the bridesmaids...."

Damn! Will fidgeted and fumed while the photographer took a mile of film, snapping and snapping at the row of bridesmaids. Will just stared at one of them—Cecily, with her hair up in a casual knot, strands falling around her face and sprayed so they'd stay there. He'd like to see her without the spray, would like to take her hair down, brush it, run his fingers through it.

She was spectacular in the white dress, holding a bouquet of white flowers—too stunning for words. He wanted to touch her, to kiss her, to tell her that whatever else went wrong with this wedding, they'd be all right.

What he really wanted to do was take the dress off.

She was gazing at him, too, and her lips parted as if she'd read his mind.

It almost did him in. He took a step toward her.

"Groomsmen."

Will froze.

"The best man isn't with us yet, so we'll skip the group photo and start pairing you guys up with bridesmaids for individual photos."

Will literally snatched Cecily out of the line of bridesmaids. It might be his only chance.

"That's right, Will and Cecily, you'll be opposite each other in the line. Muffy, you'll have to wait for a photo with Derek because he's late getting here. Will, stand beside Cecily, but a little behind her…"

*And speak directly into her left ear.* "Cecily, we'll have to say our goodbyes now."

"…hand on her elbow, Will, not around her shoulders…good, good…"

"I have a plan, sort of," she said out of the side of her mouth. "Can you come up to Vermont next weekend?"

"No," he said. "I have to work. But…"

"Would you be free for the Memorial Day weekend?" She was starting to sound sad, while his elation was growing by leaps and bounds. She didn't want to tell him goodbye.

"I don't know exactly where I'll be on Memorial Day, but…"

"Fourth of July?"

He yawned. "It's hard to travel over the Fourth of July."

"Labor Day?" She was starting to sound desperate. That was good.

"It's a little far ahead to schedule Labor Day."

"So I suppose it's way too far ahead to schedule Thanksgiving."

"Straighten up, you two. Smile, Cecily. You look like you've seen a ghost. That's right. Nice smile…"

"Are you telling me goodbye—for good?" Cecily asked him, smiling maniacally.

"No, I was thinking how much easier it would be if I—"

"Look at the camera, please, Will, and stop moving your lips, both of you."

Will hissed through closed, curved lips. "—if I moved to Vermont. Then I wouldn't have to do all that traveling."

"What?" She spun to face him.

The photographer heaved an exasperated sigh. "Can we have a little cooperation here?"

Cecily turned toward the camera again, and Will decided not to keep her dangling. "I've decided to resign from the firm. I'll set up my own office. In Vermont, if you'll have me. You may have to support me financially while I get the business up and running." He was exaggerating here, but he thought it sounded good.

"But Will, is that what you want? A small office instead of a high-powered, well-staffed one?" she spoke with her mouth skewed to one side.

"Is she having a stroke?" the photographer moaned.

"That's the choice I'm making," Will said, soft and low. "I can't lie and I can't do damage to the people I love. It will take me a month or so to wrap things up, but I'm going to hand over Gus's tax business to a colleague and welcome Gus into the family, who-ever, whatever, he is. If Sally loves him, that's enough for me." He moved in a little closer. "And if you think you could learn to love me, I'll move anywhere."

"Oh, Will." Cecily seemed to forget they weren't alone. She turned and gazed into his eyes. "I think there's a strong chance, a very strong chance, I might." Her eyes shone. "You would really do this to be close to me?"

"Come on, people, let me get one decent shot before you…"

"Can't help myself," Will said. "You're just too great in bed. Gotta have you." He smiled as he folded his arms around her and she came to him, face up-turned, lips parted.

"I give up," the photographer said disgustedly. "I'll shoot somebody else first."

"This wedding is nuts." That was Paula Perry, get-ting dramatic. "Everybody's missing or late or mad or falling in love. Does *anybody* know if Gus is back yet?"

"Gus who?" Will said. His mouth moved down to-ward Cecily's waiting one, and in front of the entire wedding party, he kissed her.

*Piper's Sex Hotel!!!!*

Heire$$ **Piper Devon**'s new Manhattan boutique hotel is all about SEX!!! Construction has begun on the deluxe spa/hotel and those in the know say the theme is sex, sex and more sex! Private video cameras in every room! A lounge with exotic dancers! Massages (with extras) 24/7! The name is HUSH, but there's no way she's keeping this a secret. What will her billionaire daddy have to say about this??? Can't wait to hear....

—Published August 2004
*National World Observer*

# 1

"WELCOME TO HUSH."

Piper Devon gazed at the crowd of photographers and journalists gathered in front of her, here to get a preview of her new boutique hotel. As she stood on a makeshift platform at the far end of the lobby, flashbulbs were popping all around her, but she didn't even blink. She'd grown up in the glare of the paparazzi, and for the first time she was able to use them for something she cared about. Her baby. Her hotel.

"Hey, Piper." She recognized one of the reporters from the *New York Post*. "Where's the sex?"

She laughed. Her photo-op laugh. "Keep your pants on, Josh." She leaned forward just a smidge, enough to give the front row a money shot. "At least until we get upstairs."

That got her exactly the response she was looking for. This time she needed the tabloids, needed them to spread the word that Hush was going to be the hottest ticket in town. That it was the place to stay in Manhattan.

One thing she'd learned in her years in the spotlight was that sex sells. Sex sells a lot. And she was the ideal spokeswoman.

"Does your father approve, Piper?"

She kept on smiling. "My father isn't exactly who I built this hotel for."

More laughter from the press. "Who did you build it for, Piper?"

She fluttered her eyelashes at the Channel 7 reporter. "For everyone who understands that Manhattan is for lovers. People who come to Hush want to explore their sexuality. Hopefully in the company of someone, well, close, but hey, there's plenty of fun to be had for the single adventurer."

"A vibrator in every room?"

"Better than a chicken in every pot, right, Elizabeth?"

The crowd of reporters laughed again. Good, excellent. "Okay, if you don't have a brochure yet, you can pick one up on your way to the elevator. We're going up to the twentieth floor, to the spa. And I promise I won't get started without you."

Her staff, all in the Hush uniform of black tuxedos with pink ties, ushered the press to the four elevators.

She shivered with anticipation as the photographers clicked away. She'd dreamed this space, and it was now a reality. The glistening lacquered reservation desk with the same shiny surface on the back wall, broken only by the pink neon art-deco Hush signage was perfection. The custom-designed furniture would have been at home in a grand salon of the 1920s. The artwork, vintage works by the likes of Erté and Bernard Villemot, was the pièce de résistance.

No one walking into this hotel would mistake it for one of the Devon hotels. It wasn't like the Orpheus, her father's flagship hotel and corporate headquarters, which was opulent to the point of nausea. No, this was a hotel for the young. The rich.

She stepped down from the podium, ready for the next part of the tour. Janice Foster, the general manager of the hotel, came up behind her, clapping her hands with excitement. "They love it. Oh, God, this is so fabulous. I heard the reporter from *Vanity Fair* say she's going to book herself a three-day weekend."

"What's not to love?" Piper said, taking Janice's arm as they walked to the elevator. "By this time next week there won't be a soul above ten who hasn't heard of Hush."

# Brenda Jackson

### and Silhouette Desire
### present a hot new romance
### starring another sexy
### Westmoreland man!

# JARED'S COUNTERFEIT FIANCÉE

### (Silhouette Desire #1654)

When debonair attorney
Jared Westmoreland needed a date,
he immediately thought of the beautiful
Dana Rollins. Reluctantly, Dana fulfilled
his request, and the two were somehow
stuck pretending that they were engaged!
With the passion quickly rising between
them, would Jared's faux fiancée turn
into the real deal?

*Available May 2005 at your favorite retail outlet.*

If you enjoyed what you just read,
then we've got an offer you can't resist!

# Take 2 bestselling love stories FREE!

# Plus get a FREE surprise gift!

# eHARLEQUIN.com
## The Ultimate Destination for Women's Fiction

The ultimate destination for women's fiction.
Visit eHarlequin.com today!

### GREAT BOOKS:
- We've got something for everyone—and at great low prices!
- Choose from new releases, backlist favorites, Themed Collections and preview upcoming books, too.
- Favorite authors: Debbie Macomber, Diana Palmer, Susan Wiggs and more!

### EASY SHOPPING:
- Choose our convenient "bill me" option. No credit card required!
- Easy, secure, 24-hour shopping from the comfort of your own home.
- Sign-up for free membership and get $4 off your first purchase.˙
- Exclusive online offers: FREE books, bargain outlet savings, hot deals.

### EXCLUSIVE FEATURES:
- Try Book Matcher—finding your favorite read has never been easier!
- Save & redeem Bonus Bucks.
- Another reason to love Fridays—Free Book Fridays!

## Shop online
## at www.eHarlequin.com today!

INTBB204

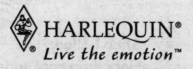

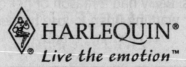

**Silhouette®**

# Desire.

**Enjoy the launch of Maureen Child's NEW miniseries**

# THREE-WAY WAGER

*The Reilly triplets bet they could go ninety days without sex. Hmmm.*

## The Tempting Mrs. Reilly
## by MAUREEN CHILD

(Silhouette Desire #1652)
Available May 2005

Brian Reilly had just made a bet to not have sex for three months when his stunningly sexy ex-wife blew into town. It wasn't long before Tina had him contemplating giving up his wager and getting her back. But the tempting Mrs. Reilly had a reason of her own for wanting Brian to lose his bet... to give her a baby!